MY NAME IS
Layla

Reyna Marder Gentin

Relax. Read. Repeat.

MY NAME IS LAYLA
By Reyna Marder Gentin
Published by TouchPoint Press
Brookland, AR 72417
www.touchpointpress.com

ISBN: 978-1-952816-08-6

Editor: Jenn Haskin
Cover Design: Colbie Myles
Cover images: Adobe Stock

Visit the author's website at reynamardergentin.com

First Edition

Printed in the United States of America

For all the dedicated teachers who inspire their students every day to reach higher,

And for Pierre, Ariella, and Micah, who teach me every day what it's all about.

*"The more that you read, the more things you will know.
The more that you learn, the more places you'll go."*
—Dr. Seuss

Chapter One

My brother Nick knows a lot about what he calls "escaping." And he doesn't mind sharing his hard-won wisdom with me, his kid sister. In fact, he considers it his responsibility. I guess I should be grateful that someone is looking out for me. He's trying, anyway.

I allow the screen door to bang shut behind me, a bowl of mac & cheese in my right hand and glass of unearthly blue Gatorade in my left. The air has that sudden chill that always arrives out of nowhere during the first week of September to warn you that school is about to start. I'm going into eighth grade and the weather feels downright frosty.

"Dinner is served," I say, planting myself carefully on the top step of the porch and balancing my drink on the railing. "There's more inside."

Nick is sitting in the rocking chair, staring into space and humming some old Coldplay tune. He's wearing a worn orange Knicks tank and grey sweats, his long legs stretched out in front of him. He needs a shave and his eyes look kind of empty, zoned out. Pretty typical Nick, especially when he's taking a break from his video games but he still doesn't feel like interacting with the world.

So I'm surprised when he suddenly sits up straight and gets all animated, speaking sort of loudly, like this is advice I really need to hear.

"The thing is, 'munk—if you need to think and get your head straight, the best way is to drive. The open road," he says dreamily. "You just pick up the keys and go. Head north on the highway and before you know it, you are in the middle of frigging Connecticut—just make sure you've got money for gas." He almost resembles an adult for a second.

"I'm thirteen, Nick, remember? I can't hit the open road."

Nick sighs. "Yeah. That sucks." He gets up from the chair in one fluid motion. If he wasn't a jock, he might've been a dancer, he's that graceful. Not like me. I'm fast but jittery.

"There are other ways to escape, 'munk," he says. He turns his back on me and walks into the house. I can hear him scraping the rest of the macaroni from the pot, singing softly to himself. "When I ruled the world..."

At home, I've always been called "'munk," short for Chipmunk. I was small and cute when the whole thing started, but there's a lot more to it than that. Total strangers tell me that my given name, Layla, is "beautiful," "poetic," "lyrical" even. But it was "given" by my father, a big

Eric Clapton fan who turned out to be a big disappointment, to put it mildly. My mom can barely say my name, it reminds her so much of him. So 'munk stuck.

I pick at my macaroni, separating out the wagon wheel shape first, then the spirals, and finally the classic elbows. I always eat it in that order. I like to think of myself not as a picky eater, but a precise eater. I'm so caught up in my food that I don't register Sammy until he's in his third lap biking around the block. When I look up, he gives me a wave. Not a super enthusiastic, "I'm so glad to see you wave," but not a half-baked, "I'd wave at anything breathing" wave either. Just a wave.

Sammy and I aren't friends, and we aren't not friends either. He's just the boy across the street who happens to be in my grade at school. My mom says that when we were little, we used to play together, but I don't have any memory of that, and I think it probably isn't true. She maybe likes to say it because it makes her look like one of those non-working moms who set up playdates—and I don't think she ever did. Plus she's always working.

I don't know all that much about Sammy or his family either, except that they're everything we aren't. The dad has a nine-to-five job that he goes to in a fancy-looking suit, and the mom stays home and takes care of Sammy and his younger brother and sister. Nobody ever looks hungry, and you can tell their clothes smell like flowers in a meadow, even from across the street. They have dinner every night together as a family at 6:30 p.m.—I can see them at their table through the picture window—and I'm betting that they discuss current events and also something special that happened to each of them during the day. The lawn is mowed, and the lights are out by 10 p.m.

"Sammy, come in for dinner!" There's nothing glamorous about Sammy's mom. She doesn't rock her mom jeans, but she seems to be totally comfortable in her clothes and in her life. She waves at me too, and her wave says, "Hi, Layla. What are you doing eating mac and cheese by yourself on your porch on the night before the first day of eighth grade?" I have no answer, so I get up and go inside. I don't wave back.

"Do you think in most families the mom makes dinner before the first day of school?" I ask Nick, who's finished the pasta and moved on to a huge bowl of ice cream.

"Mom is working, 'munk. You should be grateful she has a job instead of whining that you're not eating a home-cooked meal. *You-know-who* certainly isn't contributing to our upkeep."

My dad is kind of like Voldemort—no one says his name either. He's always referred to as "You-know-who." He left when I was a baby and has yet to reappear. His real name is Jeff.

"I know she's working," I say. "But couldn't she trade shifts with someone so she could be here with us on important nights?" My mom's an emergency room nurse at the local hospital. Her shift is 7 p.m. to 7 a.m., and then she comes home and sleeps during the day. She works three nights in a row, the max, and then often works overtime for the extra cash. On the days she's off, her sleep cycle is so turned around she barely functions. But she does keep us in this house with food, such as it is, on the table.

"What's so special about tonight?" Nick asks, shoveling another spoonful of Rocky Road into his mouth and then talking as he crunches on the nuts. "You're going into eighth grade. That's not exactly earth shattering. You need to chill."

Nick does "chill" better than anyone. Nothing bothers him. And I know he's right. I mean, he's going to be a senior. That's a pretty big deal. I'm just in for another meaningless year of middle school, boring teachers, mediocre grades, awkward social situations. Still, the whole concept of a hearty meal, and a good night's sleep, and new clothes carefully chosen and laid out on the chair—it has a certain appeal.

"Yeah, I'm sure you're right," I say. I turn on my computer and binge watch four episodes of *How I Met Your Mother*.

Earlier today was classic Mom. When she got up in the late afternoon from her "night's" sleep, she wandered into my room. I was combing through my t-shirts, trying to figure out what to wear tomorrow. She flopped down on my bed and watched me for a few minutes, like I was some exotic animal in the zoo that she hadn't seen before. Like when they had the new pandas in Washington D.C.

"Have you picked something out, 'munk?" Mom asked. I looked at the neat piles in front of me. I wanted to ask her if she remembered when she was my age how important it was to have something new to wear on the first day of school. But I didn't want to make her feel bad, so I just said "no."

I held up some different options, looking at myself in the mirror while Mom sat on my bed, saying nothing.

After a while I think she couldn't stand it anymore, because she sounded kind of impatient when she finally said, "Do you have to wear a shirt with some kind of slogan emblazoned across your chest? Wouldn't it be better to wear something plain and pretty, and make your own statement?"

I looked at the shirts I'd been considering – "Krispy Kreme Donuts," "Taylor Swift," "Bart Simpson." I guess she had a point. But then I thought about the words that the teachers would see written on a blank slate, if not tomorrow, then soon enough: "Lazy," "Underachiever," "Unmotivated," "Daydreamer." No, a ready-made saying was safer. I pulled out the Guns 'n Roses t-shirt Nick bought me at the concert he went to over the summer. I don't know any of their songs, but at least it's new. "This one's good," I said. Mom sighed, and got up to get ready for work.

Before I get into bed, I brush my long dark hair out in front of the mirror and tie it back loosely, wishing I had dyed a section blue or purple or something cool for the new year. But mom never would've let me, so I didn't ask. I stare at my reflection for a moment. My hair is definitely my best feature. It's shiny and straight and reaches almost to my waist. I remember how freaked out I was in third grade when a bunch of the girls in my class had lice and I thought I'd have to cut my hair if I got it too, but then I didn't. The rest of my face is kind of ordinary. Brown eyes, standard nose, acne on a monthly basis. At least I never had to have braces.

When I get underneath my quilt and the room is dark and quiet, I text Liza, my best friend.

"Can't believe this whole thing is starting all over again," I type.

"It'll be okay, Layla. Eighth grade—WE RULE THE SCHOOL! Mom says I need to crash now," Liza answers.

I have a pang of jealousy that Liza's mom cares what time she goes to bed, but I don't let on.

"K. Let's meet out front and walk in together," I type.

7

Reyna Marder Gentin

I'm glad she knows without any explanation that I need moral support. It would be too embarrassing if she were anyone else. After going to this school for so long, I should be able to walk in the door by myself on the first day—but Liza's so nice, she'd never make fun of me for it.

"Sure," she says. "See you at 8:30 by the flagpole. Go to bed."

At least Liza tells me when to go to sleep.

Nick says I don't appreciate how hard Mom works just to keep us afloat. But it's not true. I just need more. I need her to be *more*.

Chapter Two

ast night I had that dream I have when something stressful is coming up, like the start of school or a test or a big homework assignment.

It's always the same. I'm sitting in the kitchen after school eating a peanut butter sandwich with the crust carefully removed and no messy jelly. There's a knock on the door and I don't race to answer it, because I think it's Nick and I'm annoyed that he forgot his key and is making me get up.

When I eventually go to the door, I look through the window and I know that the man standing there is my dad, even though I haven't really ever met him, if you don't count when I was a baby. He looks like me, or I look like him, and there's no question who he is. For some reason, I let him in.

And this is where the dream gets really strange. My dad sits down and after a few minutes of polite small talk, he tells me that he has come to solve all my problems. I know that sounds crazy, but in the dream I tell him a lot of stuff about school and about mom, and he's really focused and listening. And then he comes up with a plan for how to fix it all.

I know, nuts. I'm not proud of it. I always wake up all shivery, even when it's really warm in my bedroom.

*D*espacito . . ."

My alarm goes off at 6:45 a.m., Luis Fonsi reminding me, loud as a screeching fire engine, to take things slowly. *No worries, hermano.* It's not like I'm jumping out of bed, wildly excited to start another school year. I've given myself exactly half an hour to get ready before my bus comes. Mom will just be leaving the hospital for home as that big yellow monster wheezes down the street, dragging me away to Hollow Hills Middle School.

I'm getting dressed and I'm feeling mostly recovered from the Dad dream when I glance in the mirror on the back of my bedroom door and notice my customary lousy posture. Immediately, I hear Liza's voice in my head.

"Stand up straight, Layla! You're slouching!"

And, of course, I am. I don't mean to slouch—I try to remember to focus, throwing my shoulders back, lifting my chin, sticking my chest out. But the truth is, with my head down, I'm able to navigate the world looking at my feet. Which I find is sometimes the safest option.

I come down the first few stairs from my bedroom standing tall and proud. Then I just feel silly, like some puffed-out version of myself, and I go back to normal. I'm heading full speed to the kitchen to grab a granola bar on my way out the door, when I run smack into Mom in the foyer.

"'munk! Slow down! And look up once in a while—you're missing stuff by staring at your Keds!"

Mom looks tired, her make-up long worn off, standing there in her blue hospital scrubs and dorky white sneakers, but she manages a big, encouraging smile.

"What're you doing home so early?" I say, confirming on my cell that it is 7:12. She isn't due to be here for another eighteen minutes; fifteen minutes after I'm gone. I don't mean to sound like I'm accusing her of something, but I know I do.

"I asked my supervisor if I could leave early, so I could catch you before you left for your first day of school," she answers, sounding a little hurt, and reaches out to give me a hug. She puts her arms around my waist and tries to pull me toward her, but our faces somehow get in the way. It's weird now that we are the same height; like I used to fit better, and now I don't. I back away immediately.

It's awkward. We aren't normally too touchy feely with each other, and besides, I just wasn't expecting her here. I appreciate the gesture and all, but my bus is coming—I can hear it now down the street.

"I gotta go, Mom. Have a good sleep, okay?" I grab my backpack off the floor next to the door, and run out, head bowed.

Only when I slump into my seat do I realize that I forgot the granola bar. My stomach growls and I silently curse Mom for distracting me from my mission.

I step off the bus and see Liza waiting by the flagpole, exactly as we've planned. She's the most reliable person I know. She puts the "best" in "best friend."

"Hey," I say. Don't get the wrong impression; I'm not some sort of social pariah and Liza isn't my only friend. But if I were stranded on a deserted island...

"Hey, yourself," Liza says. "You look nice." I know I look okay, like I haven't done anything weird with my clothes or my hair, but I understand the subtext—you look nice, Layla, even though you didn't get to go shopping for something new. Don't worry about it; it's not that important.

"Thanks," I say. "I like your shoes," I add, because they're screaming, '*I just came out of the box!,*' and they are really cool and Liza deserves to be happy and excited about the start of a new school year.

We push our way through the front doors of the building, kids jostling, hugging, high-fiving.

"Do you think there will ever be a day when I don't feel a little nauseous going up these steps?" I ask.

Liza shakes her head. "Probably not."

That's what I love about Liza. No bull, or no "sugar coating" as she'd say, which is an expression she picked up from her grandma, because Liza speaks in a nicer way than I do. I shove her shoulder with mine, and as she's regaining her balance in her new shoes, I scamper up the long flight of marble steps in my trusty Keds, not giving myself any opportunity to stall further.

We meet up at our lockers. This is going to sound stupid, but my locker is like the oasis in the desert of my middle school. One of the few cool things about this place is that you're assigned a locker in sixth grade and you get to keep it all the way until graduation day in eighth. Not only that, you can decorate it with photographs and things you cut out from magazines, and because it's yours for the whole three years, the school doesn't take anything down over the summer. You just have to clean out the food and anything else that might get gross. My locker is a time machine. I can look back and see what geeky actor I thought was hot in sixth grade, or which group of girls I took those goofy photo booth pics with last year even though I hardly talk to them anymore.

The best thing is that my locker is right next to Liza's. That's how we met.

I do the combination, and the cast of "Hamilton on Broadway" smiles back at me. I didn't actually see the show, but I know every word of every song by heart. All of the walls of my locker are covered, collage style, and I wonder where I will have room to add anything this year. I stick my whole head in to examine whether I could tape some stuff up on the ceiling.

While I'm admiring my own artwork, Liza has put her notebooks and new textbooks neatly into her locker. Her decoration scheme is more streamlined than mine. She has a formal looking photo of her family at a fancy wedding, a couple of glossy pics of Justin Bieber, and a small whiteboard where she leaves herself reminders of stuff she needs to do. She's a way better student than I am too. But she doesn't make me feel bad about it.

"Come on, let's go—we both have McCarthy for English first period," Liza says. *How does she do that?* I can barely keep track of my own schedule, but she always seems to know where she's supposed to be and where I'm supposed to be.

"Yes, Ma'am," I say, sticking out my tongue at her. But the truth is I'm grateful whenever Liza is in class with me. She's really good at knowing what the homework is and when its due, and she doesn't seem to mind when I ask her stuff over and over again because I didn't manage to write down the assignments.

We settle into two seats in the front row—again, something I'd never do, but with Liza there, it's okay. McCarthy is a young guy, new to the school this year. His face is a little pink with how hard he's trying.

"I just want you to know," he says, looking earnest and silly all at once, "that I'm here for you, if you ever have any questions about what we're reading or studying. Or even just about how to deal with middle school—nothing will freak me out. I mean, I'm not that much older than you guys." He smiles broadly, and he certainly does look young. But I'm not sure where he falls on the phony meter—I mean, maybe he thinks he's supposed to say stuff like that, and really he'll be just as tough on me as the teachers always are.

Done with his intro speech, McCarthy turns on the smartboard, which has a quote from *Of Mice and Men*, which we were supposed to read over the summer. I had to read it like three times before I got that there was something wrong with Lennie and that George was taking care of him. Liza is always telling me that I'm smart, but she doesn't get what it's like in my head. Like now, for instance. McCarthy's got a quote up there and it's something about rabbits, but no matter how slowly I go over it in my head, it isn't making sense. The words hop around like any good bunny should, refusing to stay still so I can get a grip on what they mean.

"Who would like to read this quote out loud for the class?" McCarthy asks. No one volunteers, not even Liza, because that would look like a majorly kiss-up thing to do, especially on the first day of school.

McCarthy scans the front row before letting his eyes land on me. Luckily, he doesn't know our names yet, so when I stare at my feet, he's kind of left in the lurch.

"I can read the quote, Mr. McCarthy."

I let out a breath and peek behind me to where the voice came from, and Sammy is looking at the smart board, concentrating as though it's some big hardship to read the one-line quote. Except for me, it is. It isn't like I don't know how to read. But with the pressure of everyone staring at me and waiting, the letters just don't form themselves into words.

So this year starts off just like every other year. Nick would tell me to chill, but I just can't seem to follow his advice.

Chapter Three

McCarthy is finally done tormenting us with *Of Mice and Men* and we've moved on to *The Outsiders*. He says it's cool because it's a book about teenagers written by a teenager. But when I was reading, I kept getting lost in all the names of the kids and which ones belonged in which gang. It reminded me of that movie *West Side Story*. Mom and I watched it one afternoon last winter when she was home with the flu. We lay in her bed under the covers, something we hadn't done since I was little, and Mom knew the words to all the songs, and she sang them quietly while the movie played. She has a pretty voice. I asked her how come I was allowed to lie so close to her when she was sick—I thought she should know better since she's a nurse. But she told me it would be okay because I had a flu shot. Which made no sense, because she had a flu shot too.

"Earth to Layla, Earth to Layla…" McCarthy is standing in front of me, and I can hear kids giggling. I shoot him as much of a death stare as I dare, because he isn't usually mean and that was a nasty thing to do to me.

Then I look up at him, all sincere with wide-eyes, and say, "I'm sorry, Mr. McCarthy, I was thinking about the book and I got lost in my imagination for a minute."

"Well, as long as you were thinking about the book," he says. "What I was saying is that I know you guys have a different social experience here at Hollow Hills than Ponyboy—you may not feel like you can relate to his world." McCarthy smiles, and I wonder if he's got much of a clue about what goes on in some of these kids' homes. I know a little, because even though Mom would never name names, she's told me that there are kids who come through the ER where she works for all different reasons, and not every injury is accidental. But I catch myself daydreaming again and try to focus on what McCarthy is saying.

"So for homework tonight, I'd like you to write something—not polished, just what comes to mind—about a time in your life when you felt like an 'outsider.' You won't have to share with the class if you choose not to, so really try to hook into the emotions and write from your heart. If you can relate your experience to Ponyboy's, that's great; but if you can't, that's fine too. A page or two is plenty. I just want you to connect to that experience."

I can hear Callie sniggering in the back. Her parents own the Mercedes dealership in town and she's always buying food and fancy hair clips for her friends because she can. She's by far the most popular girl in my grade, and everyone can tell she's thinking she's never had an outsider moment in her life. Even McCarthy, who can be pretty clueless, gets what's going on.

"Callie, everyone has situations where they don't quite fit in. If you think hard enough, I have confidence that you'll come up with at least one," McCarthy says. "Please email the assignment to me by 10 p.m. tonight." Then he dismisses the class.

"What do you think McCarthy would do if someone used this homework to confess to having some real problem?" I ask Liza quietly as we put our books and binders in our backpacks.

"I think he would try to help," Liza says, looking at me with her eyebrows raised. "Don't you?"

"I'm not sure," I say. But it's okay. I don't plan on finding out.

I sit down on the living room couch after dinner with my laptop and try to come up with some harmless and not too personal outsider moment to share with nosy McCarthy. Something he'll find "authentic," as he says too often, but that has nothing to do with what actually makes me an outsider even to myself: that sometimes my brain doesn't work right and I can't make sense of what I'm reading or writing. I think about Ponyboy, and I wonder whether he likes his name. I mean, Pony is short for Ponyboy – just like 'munk is short for Chipmunk. But the guy who wrote the book made a point of explaining that

Ponyboy was his legit name on his birth certificate. I can't imagine that. I might be an outsider in a lot of ways, but at least my real name is something normal.

It's 9:45 p.m. I've written nothing, or at least nothing coherent. I've rambled on about being an outsider because Mom has a very demanding job that keeps her away from home a lot, but I certainly haven't mentioned You-know-who. All I need is McCarthy deciding I come from a broken home. But when I go back to read the couple of paragraphs I've managed to write, some of the words don't make sense. And the spell check is a total fail, because even the computer can't figure out what I'm trying to say.

"Well if that's the way you want it," I say, in my tough girl voice, and then I type out the next page and a half. Except I type wherever my fingers land, total nonsense. It's strangely satisfying. Although I feel that tingling thing in my nose when I'm about to cry.

"Screw you, McCarthy," I mutter. I hit the send button before I can have second thoughts. I slam my laptop shut and I go upstairs to find Nick.

When I get to the landing, the music coming out of Nick's bedroom is so loud that within seconds my jaw is throbbing to the beat of Maroon Five. How could I not have heard it from downstairs? I bang on the door, but Nick doesn't answer.

Nick is sitting cross-legged on the floor in his boxer briefs and one of those sleeveless white tanks he and his friends call "wife beaters," the controller from his Xbox in one hand and a donut in the other, a few still left in the open box on the floor.

"Hey, 'munk! Ever think about knocking?" he says, but he isn't really mad. "You want a donut?" His eyes are vacant after too many hours of playing video games and texting with his friends, but the kindness is still there.

"No, I'm good," I say, flopping myself down on the bed. "How many of those have you had?" I ask.

"I'm not sure. Not that many. Maybe this is my second? The sugar helps me play better—amps up my reflexes." Nick looks confused by the effort of thinking and counting. I count backwards from the dozen that the box started with and figure out he's scarfed down five.

"You're not going to believe what I just did," I say, even though I realize that he's way checked out and living in his own virtual reality. He'd probably believe just about anything. But I need to talk to someone.

"I just submitted an English assignment, but I thought the teacher was asking too many personal questions, so I just made up gibberish words. The whole thing was garbage." I look at Nick to see whether I've gone too far, even for him. His eyes crinkle up and he starts to laugh. He laughs so much I'm afraid he'll keel over, but it's contagious. In a minute I'm laughing so hard myself I'm afraid I may pee my pants.

Tears come to my eyes, and then I'm just straight out crying—I'm not sure what happened to the laughing, but it's like it disappeared. Except Nick is still laughing, and now that's making me mad. He finally notices what's going on, and he says, "Aw, c'mon, 'munk, come sit down by me." He pats the floor next to him, and I go and sit by his side, moving the donut box out of the way. I lean up against him and put my head on his shoulder.

"It's okay," Nick says. "It isn't that big a deal." And then he offers me the Xbox controller. "Play for a little while. You'll see, it's a great escape."

I've never been much into video games—the music's too loud for me, and the games Nick plays are so violent. And he's obsessed with them, sitting by himself, playing for hours every night after he finishes his homework. But Nick looks way more chill than I feel. And he's my brother and I know he loves me. So I take the controller and I try to smash whatever is coming at me, but it's all too fast and after a minute I put my hands over my eyes and duck my head down, dropping the controller on the floor.

And then I wail as hard as I was laughing a few minutes before, and I think I will never breathe again. It's like the crying somehow clears my vision, because now I see that Nick doesn't look mellow or chill sitting on his bedroom floor. He looks brain dead. Sweet, as always, but brain dead. I get to my feet.

"Thanks, Nick, but I don't think this way of escaping is going to work for me," I say. I muss the top of his head. "Promise me you won't sit here playing this all night," I say. Remembering his number one method of clearing his head I add, "Why don't you go take a drive?"

"I promise," he says. "I'm not addicted to these games, you know. I just need to smooth things out for myself sometimes." But I'm not sure.

I leave his room, closing the door behind me, and head down to the kitchen. I might as well fortify myself before going to sleep. Tomorrow could be a long day.

Chapter Four

I wake up the next morning a full five minutes before my alarm, Nick tickling my feet where they are sticking out from my quilt. I tend to thrash around at night, throwing my sheets and blankets off, knocking my pillows onto the floor. My nighttime mischief upsets me, because when I'm awake, I like things neat and orderly. Mom says that she pities whoever has to sleep with me someday, which is not such a nice thing to say, but I get what she means.

Nick is standing at the foot of my bed, "coochy-cooing" my toes, and I'm doing my best to kick him in the knees or the privates, wherever I happen to hit.

"You look like you stayed up all night with those stupid games," I say, giggling despite my best efforts to look pissed off.

"Nah, this is how I always look in the morning. You just don't usually see me before I drive to school." Nick has stepped away from my bed and is examining himself in the mirror. He seems pleased with what he sees, striking some pose that is meant to look cool, but in my bedroom just looks silly.

"What do you want?" I ask, since it's true that he's normally gone before I get out of bed.

"To make sure you go to school. You know, to face the music." He runs his fingers through his hair to get just the right messy look, and then wipes the excess gel on my arm.

For a second I'm not sure what he means. And then it comes rushing back to me—my little rebellion, my gobbledygook homework assignment. McCarthy's face floats in front of my eyes, and my mouth goes dry. I'm not afraid of a bad grade—I'm used to that. I just can't stand that part where I have to sit and talk to him. Because you know that's coming.

"It'll be okay," Nick says. "Remember, no one messes with my little sister." And he pulls what remains of my bedding off of me, tossing it onto the floor with the rest. Before I can lay a hand on him, he's gone—so fast on his feet that I don't stand a chance.

Hey, why are you walking so slow?" Sammy says as he catches up and then almost passes me by in the hallway on the way to English.

"Guess I'm not the teacher's pet you are, racing to be the first to class," I answer, but I smile, so he'll know I'm kidding.

He slows his pace and walks with me and I can't imagine why until he takes a deep breath and starts talking. The words come out in a rapid stream as though he might lose his nerve somewhere mid-sentence if he slows down.

"So I was wondering whether maybe you might want to go to the homecoming game Friday night with me?" Sammy hasn't looked at me once, but I have a good view of his profile. He's pretty cute in a geeky sort of way. His hair is cut a little too short, but it's a nice color, like a Twix bar, and his nose is nice and straight.

I'm so caught off guard that I don't answer at first or even acknowledge that Sammy's asked me a question. And then I realize it isn't really a question—he's asked me on a date. No one's ever asked me on a date before. Maybe I should take some time to think about it, but I plunge right in.

"I'm already going to homecoming," I say. "My brother's on the basketball team."

"Everyone knows Nick," Sammy says, smiling and finally turning toward me.

And it's true. Everyone does know Nick. He's been on the varsity basketball team since ninth grade, when he'd already hit six feet. Nick was a natural then, and he's only gotten better. He should be the captain. The guys on the team are completely devoted to him, especially the younger ones, because when he's not sitting like lump in front of his Xbox, he works at his game. He's unfailingly fair, and he's always encouraging and never mean. But Coach says he has some maturing to do.

No kidding.

Thinking about Nick I don't notice that we've reached the classroom and I haven't exactly responded to Sammy's invitation. But when we go inside, the lights are out and it's weird, and I forget what we'd been talking about. For a second I have this strange sensation that it's dark because the class is throwing me a surprise birthday party, and then I remember it's October and my birthday's in February.

"Come in, you're the last two. Sit down so we can start," McCarthy says. "I thought we'd take a little break from all the yapping and watch the movie adaptation of *The Outsiders*. We won't finish because it's too long, but I think you'll enjoy it."

If I could kiss McCarthy at that moment, I would. There's nothing I like better than seeing a movie when I've tried to read the book first and I know I haven't understood everything. I settle into my seat, forget all about Sammy, and let the Greasers and the Socs duke it out on the smart board. McCarthy is right—the rivalries make a lot more sense when I can see the characters, and I can feel my face burning when Pony misses his curfew by accident and his brother, who's supposed to be taking care of him, hits him. I'm totally caught up when McCarthy turns off movie and the bell hasn't even rung yet.

"Hey, what're you doing?" I demand, and even Liza laughs at how angry I am.

"Glad you're enjoying the movie, Layla," McCarthy says, smiling like the Cheshire cat who swallowed the canary, or whatever that stupid expression is. "I need a couple of minutes to hand back yesterday's assignment." And then it's like the whole last 45 minutes of pleasure was leading up to this one moment of doom. I slouch down in my chair.

I can hear McCarthy talking, but he sounds the way the adults do in those old Charlie Brown cartoons—"wah wah wah wah, wah, wah wah." I catch snippets—"thanks for being so honest," and "I've really learned something about you all,"—but I know he isn't talking about me. I wish to God that I had just written some garbage about feeling like an outsider because I don't play sports or because I don't wear make-up or some other stupid thing. He totally would've bought it, and I wouldn't be in this situation. But it's too late for that now.

Then McCarthy is in front of me, holding out my paper. I don't meet his eyes, but instead take it from him and hold it close to my chest, waiting for him to move off before I slowly peel it away from my shirt and look at the grade. C+. Not nearly as bad as it could've been, and no worse than my usual grades. But it doesn't make sense, and that makes my stomach hurt.

The bell rings and then there's the sound of chairs scraping and everyone talking and grabbing their backpacks. Sammy leans over and says, "Think about Friday night," and then he practically runs out of the classroom, not nearly as suave as he would've liked, I'm sure. Before Liza has a chance to ask me what Sammy wanted or to get me moving to Earth Science, McCarthy is in front of me again.

"Layla, can you stay a couple of minutes?" he asks.

"Well, I have class now," I say, hoping somehow that Liza will come to my rescue.

"Just two minutes, and I'll give you a late pass," McCarthy says. No way to argue really. Liza throws me a sympathetic look and then abandons me. I stay in my chair while McCarthy pulls up another one a few feet away.

"So I wanted to explain the grade that I gave you on your paper," he says quietly. He sounds kind of apologetic and all "new-teacherish" and I feel bad for him.

"It's okay, Mr. McCarthy," I say. "I know you're just doing your job. And this isn't such a bad grade anyway."

"Well, I want to let you know what I was thinking, and maybe you'll be able to let me know if I'm on to something," he says. I don't like the way that sounds. Like he's doing some kind of detective work on me.

"Here's the thing. When I saw all those paragraphs of words that weren't really words, at first I thought you were making an absolutely inspired statement about being an outsider. I thought it was a metaphor—that you were saying that when an outsider tries to express herself, she isn't speaking the same language as the people around her, so she can't be understood. That something is wrong with the communication itself. I was going to give you an A." McCarthy is watching me for any reaction, but I'm way too good at this game. No way I'm revealing anything, even if, as he puts down his theory, it has what Mom would call the "ring of truth" to it.

When I don't say anything, McCarthy continues. "But then I thought some more about it, and I decided it could just be you saying, "Back off, McCarthy, I don't need your stupid assignment and I'm not telling you anything personal about me because it's none of your darn business."

And that kind of has the ring of truth too. But I just stay quiet, a stone wall.

"So I was going to give you an 'F'."

McCarthy stands up and goes to his desk and writes out a pass so I won't get into trouble in science when I show up ten minutes late. I don't tell him that my lateness will mean that I am even more lost than usual, and the whole period will be a total waste now.

"So because I can't tell if you're brilliant or just stubborn, I averaged the two grades and came up with a C+," he says, handing me the pass. "I hope if you deserved the 'A' you'll tell me and we can take it from there," McCarthy says, nodding once at me and then turning his back to write something on the smart board for his next class.

On the way to science, I take another minute to throw the C+ paper on the floor of my locker, where it lands on top of several other lousy grades from other classes, slowly accumulating until the day I'll have to gather it all together to give to mom for parent-teacher conferences. I slam the door shut and walk down the hallway.

Chapter Five

Liza and I are sprawled out on my bed, our presentation on Rosa Parks on index cards stacked in neat piles on the floor, on my pillow, on top of our library books. I love the early part of the school year when the teachers don't interfere and let you choose your own partners for projects. I always pick Liza. Not just because she's really smart, but because she understands that what I do best is come up with good ideas and make neat piles. I leave the down and dirty follow-through to her. We make a great team.

"Why do you always want to come to my house instead of yours after school?" I ask, reshuffling the pile labeled "Early Life."

"I like to take the bus," Liza answers without hesitation.

That can't be the reason. I know what it's like at Liza's in the afternoon, because once in a while I win, and we go there. It's heaven. Her mom picks her up from school every day in a minivan that still has that new car smell even though they've had it for a year. And there are cucumbers and red peppers and bananas and almonds in little glass bowls set out on the kitchen table. Her mother is a goddess of healthy snacks, and she sits with us and asks relevant questions about our teachers and stuff going on at school right now—like tryouts for the play or the controversy over the new language requirement. Liza's mom is "authentic," in the good way McCarthy means.

"Don't kid a kidder," I say, one of Nick's favorite expressions.

Liza looks up, pretends to be surprised at my mild challenge. But I've called her out, and she's too honest to keep up the lie.

"I like your freedom," she says. "It's cool that you have your own key and that no one hangs over us when we eat cold leftover pizza. And I like that I don't get the third degree about stuff that's nobody's business." This is as close as Liza gets to riled up, and I regret asking because I don't like to upset her. But it's amazing to see the flip side. I'm wondering if there's anything else about my life that Liza envies when my phone vibrates.

"Friday night?" the text reads. No preamble, but none was necessary. *Sammy.*

"What's that about?" Liza asks. It's no big deal that she's read my text over my shoulder, but it still irritates me.

"Sammy asked me to go to the homecoming game with him. It's dumb because obviously I'm going anyway," I say, but even I can hear the excitement in my voice. As great as Liza is, no one's ever asked her on a date either.

"Well, say 'yes,' you loser!" Liza grabs for my phone, but I manage to hold onto it before she can do any damage.

"What am I going to talk to him about?" I ask. If I've said more than twenty words to Sammy in the last thirteen years, it's a lot.

"Who cares?" Liza says. "He's hot! Maybe you don't have to talk at all," she says. Then she's making kind of gross slurpy sounds with her mouth that I guess are supposed to be kissing noises but sound more like when I have to use the plunger because Nick has stuffed the toilet with too much paper.

"Stop it!" I say, but I'm laughing. I go into the bathroom and shut the door, stare at my cell. And then I type, *"K."*

All week the Hollow Hills Middle School "spirit crew" has been decorating for homecoming like it's March Madness or something. It's a little weird, because the homecoming dance is only for the high school kids, but the game is for everyone and the community too. If I didn't have Nick, I don't think I'd be paying attention at all. But I do have Nick, and he's a major celebrity. Somebody has taken photos of him shooting layups and dunking and turned them into six-foot-two life-size cardboard cutouts and put them around the hallways of the middle school. When I come out of the girls' bathroom on the second floor, I almost bump into "Nick," the word "AWESOME!" floating in a cardboard bubble over his cardboard head. If they could see how he leaves dirty dishes on his bedroom floor when he's binging on Fortnite I'm not sure they'd be so impressed. But I'm proud.

When Friday arrives, Sammy and I have not said one word to each other about the game. I'm thinking he's changed his mind when he taps me on the shoulder during lunch and says, "Should my mom pick you up tonight?" I shake my head because Sammy lives across the street and it seems silly that she would "pick me up."

"No, that's okay. I'm going early with Nick to watch the team warm up," I say. Mom is going too, but she can't stay for the whole game, so she'll take her own car. "I'll save you a seat," I add, because that seems like the polite thing to do on a date.

*B*oth teams are out on the court before the tip off— Nick and the Hollow Hills Blazers in the home white uniforms, and our cross-town rivals, the Valley Lake Cougars, in red and gold. I'm sitting in the best spot in the bleachers, right on the center court line, about fifteen rows up. When Liza comes in with the rest of our posse, she strategically sits four rows behind me— far enough not to be too obvious, but close enough to watch me and Sammy. I would ask her to move, but there isn't going to be anything to watch, and the noise in the gym will certainly keep Liza from hearing anything we talk about. If we talk about anything at all.

I'm watching Nick kid around with one of the players on the Cougars, number 15—they went to basketball camp together a couple of summers ago—when Sammy sits down in the seat next to me.

"Hey," he says.

"Hey," I say back.

Sammy gives me a big smile, and I finally see what Liza's talking about.

"Man, their guys are gigantic," Sammy says, surveying the Cougars. Sammy's one of those boys who was a shrimpy five-feet at his bar mitzvah six months ago, and has grown four inches since then. There's no telling if he'll actually end up tall, but he's certainly moving in the right direction. When I focus on the other team, I see that Sammy's right.

"Yeah. They're huge. I don't think there's a kid who's under six-five," I say. Nick is 6 foot 2, and most of the Valley Lake players are a good few inches taller than he is. I must be frowning, because Sammy tries to comfort me.

"It doesn't matter," he says. "I think once you're tall, it doesn't make that much difference how tall. And besides, Nick is better than all of them." Sammy's sincere, but flattering my brother definitely would win him points even if he weren't. I smile at him, and he sits up taller. I make a mental note to smile more.

"See those guys over there?" Sammy points with his chin to three middle-aged men on the other side of the gym wearing identical gray suits, crisp white shirts, red ties, all talking animatedly into their cell phones. I'd noticed them during warm-ups, figured they were dads.

"Scouts," Sammy says.

"What? How do you know that?" I'm impressed by his confidence, but I know he could be making stuff up.

"I don't really know," he admits, "but I think so. This is a big game, and there are four seniors on each team. Makes sense that someone would scope them out."

Sammy sounds so sure that I want to believe he's right. Nick wants nothing more in the world than to win a scholarship to play ball at the college level. He doesn't care if the school's D3, or even whether he ends up on some dinky campus in the middle of a cornfield. He needs a ticket out of our tiny town where nothing ever happens, a fresh start.

It's 8:00 p.m. on the dot and Nick and his old camp buddy face off for the start, and now I'm totally absorbed, barely aware of Sammy sitting next to me except when his knee accidentally touches mine. The sound in the gym is jacked by how many people have shown up, and everyone is cheering full out each time the ball turns over and the players go racing down the court. Nick has the ball and I'm on my feet, jumping and screaming "Go! Go! Go!" so loudly there is no room for anything else in my head. He scores six times in the first half, including two three-pointers from the corner, his specialty.

"He makes those look so easy," Sammy shouts so I can hear him.

Nick has a variety of ways of escaping our small town and our not-so-ideal home situation—cars, girls, and video games among them. But he works at his game like it's his salvation.

When the buzzer sounds, Hollow Hills is beating Valley Lake by eight at the half—way too close a margin for comfort. I turn around and Liza catches my eye and gives me a "thumbs up," which I figure is probably more about Sammy than the game. I turn back around and see my mom picking up her jacket and her bag further down the bleachers. She's dressed in her scrubs so she could stay as late as possible, but now she needs to go. I wave at her but she doesn't see me. Then I watch as she goes over to Nick to say goodbye. He's standing by the water fountain in the corner of the gym, one arm around the waist of this week's girl of interest. Her name is Kiki, and she's a cheerleader. Her short skirt and pom poms are a main attraction for my brother, who is whispering in her ear, undoubtedly making a plan for after the game. I see my mother smile before she turns away and leaves the gym.

Our totally lame marching band finishes banging out its pathetic rendition of our totally lame fight song—"Go You Mighty Blazers"—and it's almost quiet enough in the gym for a conversation. Sammy looks thoughtful for a few seconds, and then gives it a try.

"What'd you think of McCarthy's test today?" he asks.

In the excitement over homecoming I had managed to push McCarthy and *The Scarlet Letter* completely out of my mind, but now they come raging back at me.

"I think I failed."

"You did not," Sammy answers. "You read the book, didn't you? The test was just that one question."

"I read most of the book, but I read kind of slow," I say, the master of understatement. "I knew I'd never finish in time, so I rented the movie on Netflix and just watched the last 15 minutes." I'm lying. I read a bunch of the book, but I watched the entire movie.

"You cheater!" he says, but he's smiling, like he admires me. I get lost in him for a minute, and then I remember the test.

"Yeah, but the test was about how the story ends— what we thought Hawthorne was trying to say by making the priest who messed with Hester die." I'm quiet a little too long, remembering my confusion and sadness when I read the question.

Sammy gives me an encouraging, "So?"

"So in the movie, the priest doesn't die. They go off into the sunset to live happily ever after in some better place together, leaving that crappy little town behind," I say.

I can see Sammy trying to work all this out in his head, and then he says something that I'm not expecting at all.

"Sometimes people who have trouble reading get extra time for assignments and tests. Or they get help from Mrs. Hirsch in the Learning Center."

Sammy looks serious and I know he's trying to be helpful, but I'm too busy trying to figure out how he knows that my grades suck and it's all I can do not to punch him in his nice, straight nose. My head is buzzing, like it's filled with bees, and I can feel my face getting as red as the Cougars' uniforms.

"So you think I'm stupid?" I blurt out, forcing myself to look him right in the eyes.

Sammy shakes his head and starts to answer and then there's a collective gasp followed by a sickening silence, like the whole gym is now focused on our conversation.

Then I hear the ref's whistle, screeching.

I look back at the court and whatever's happened is over. Cougar number 15, the kid from camp, is squatting down next to someone sprawled on the floor. And now everyone is talking in hushed whispers except Coach, who's running onto the court and yelling to the ref to call 911. And I realize that the figure on the ground is Nick and I'm charging down the bleachers, skipping steps and pushing people aside, and Sammy is trying to keep up with me but I don't care if he does.

"Did that kid hurt Nick? I'll kill him!"

"It's his knee, it's his knee," someone's yelling.

"He hit his head too, when he went down—I saw it," someone else says.

Number 15 is sitting on the court with his head in his hands, and it's pretty clear from the way everyone is consoling him that if he did run into Nick, it was an accident and not a nasty foul. Nick's on his back, kind of rolling from side to side. His eyes are bleary with pain, and he's yelling, "Mom, Mom!" like a little kid. When I reach him, he stops moving long enough to fix me with a long stare and cries out, "I need Mom!"

I say, "She left. She'll be in the ER when you get there," because I heard the siren a second ago and now there's two guys coming with a stretcher, and Mom works in the hospital closest to the school.

"You riding in the ambulance?" The paramedic looks at me, sizing me up.

"Yes, sir. I'm his sister," I say.

"I didn't figure you for his girlfriend," he says, and he winks. But I don't find it funny.

The medics put Nick on the stretcher. He reaches out and grabs my wrist, squeezes so hard it hurts.

"'munk, don't leave me!"

"I'm not leaving you," I say. But I'm as scared as he is.

41

Chapter Six

I wake up in the corner of the ER on the cot the doctors use when it gets quiet in the middle of the night and they can sleep for a few minutes. I'm still wearing one of Nick's old Blazers basketball jerseys, and someone has covered me with a light blanket. Mom strokes my hair and her fingertips feel cool on my forehead. I know it's her without opening my eyes. I wish I could stay this way a little longer.

"Time to get up, sweetie," she says. "I need to go home and get some sleep."

I open my eyes and blink at the harsh fluorescent lights above me. Mom has her hair tied back from her face the same way I wear mine, and she looks tired like she always does after a night shift. But now she seems sad and nervous too. Her shoulders are rolled forward and she's playing with the silver ring she wears on her pinky, turning it round and round.

"Where's Nick?" I ask, getting up from the cot so fast that I stumble and have to sit down again for a second. "We can't just leave him here."

"He's going to be fine," Mom says. I believe her, because she knows these things. "He's in good hands. I made sure he got assigned to Darlene—she's the prettiest nurse here."

I smile, because that's the sort of thing that would matter to Nick, if he were feeling well enough to care.

"What'd the doctor say?"

"He tore his ACL and he's going to need surgery to fix it," Mom says. "And when he went down on the court, he hit the back of his head on the gym floor and got a concussion."

"Did number 15 foul him?" I ask. I'm irrationally fixated on that kid, even though I saw with my own eyes how upset he was. Someone to blame.

"No, 'munk. No one fouled him. He was running hard toward the hoop and his body went one way and his knee went the other way. It's a common basketball injury," Mom says. "He didn't need the concussion on top of it, but your brother likes to do things big," she says, sighing.

And then it hits me. "Is he done for the season?" I can't bear to ask Mom if his chances of being recruited are over.

"He'll need to recuperate from the surgery, which they can't do until he gets over the concussion, and then do physical therapy. He's not playing anymore this year." Now Mom looks like she might cry, and I wish she weren't a nurse and didn't have to act strong and could just be a regular mom.

"Does he know?" My voice is so quiet I think she hasn't heard me. She puts her arm around my shoulders and starts to walk me toward the exit.

"There's time for that," Mom says. "His head is still pretty fuzzy. I told him we'd talk later."

But I know he's figured it out already. You can't kid a kidder.

When we get home it's already 8:00 in the morning. I can't believe how much has happened since last night when I was sitting in the bleachers cheering Nick on. I'm wide awake, having slept most of the night, but Mom is fading fast. I make us each a piece of whole wheat toast with peanut butter and sliced banana, and a mug of hot cocoa.

"Thanks, 'munk. This hits the spot," she says. Mom eats ravenously, and then her head practically lands in the plate she's so exhausted. I pull off her shoes and help her to her bed. I know I should just let Mom rest, but I can't keep the thought inside.

"He's going to be so doomed when he finds out he's done," I say, choking on the words.

"Nick will be okay," Mom says, her words already muffled by her pillow. "He's a resilient kid. You both are." And then she's out.

I hope she's right.

ith Mom dead to the world for the next seven hours and Nick lying in the hospital in painkiller la-la land, I decide to use the time alone to finish *The Scarlet Letter*. I go outside and settle myself onto one of the rocking chairs, throw a blanket over my legs. With no time pressure, I'm reading crazy slow and I still have to re-read a lot, but I'm finally getting the rhythm of it. I'm glad that the priest dies in the book, because he was a total hypocrite, but I don't really understand what it's supposed to prove about morality or religion. I'm trying to sort all that out when I see Sammy come out of his house, cross the street, and come up the steps of my porch.

"Hey," he says.

"Hey," I say. I feel a little pissed off, but I don't know why. Then I remember.

"How's Nick?" Sammy asks. "I tried to text you last night, but you didn't answer."

I think about that for a second and remember that Mom made me turn off my cell phone in the ER. I decide not to tell Sammy. Let him come to his own conclusions. But whatever Sammy's thinking he just stands there waiting for me to answer his question about Nick. So I do.

"He's going to be okay, but he ripped up his knee and he's got a concussion." I leave out the part about being done for the season. It doesn't seem right that Sammy should know that before anyone officially tells Nick. The whole thing stinks.

"Oh, wow," Sammy says. "It looked pretty bad. Coach made the team play the rest of the game, you know, for Nick. They whipped the Cougars." Sammy smiles, and somehow I do too. Then he notices my book.

"I'm sorry I said that stuff about extra time—"

"Forget it, okay?" I adjust the blanket over my legs and feel a wave of fatigue wash over me.

Sammy nods. I don't need him to remind me of how bad my situation is. As my lousy grades pile up on the floor of my locker, the moment of truth gets closer. Even Mom, who works harder than anyone, makes time to come to parent-teacher conferences at the end of the semester. The ritual of revealing what a loser student I am will play out yet again in a few weeks' time, and with all these new subjects, this may be the worst it's ever been. As much as I want Nick to come home, maybe he can stay in the hospital long enough that Mom will forget to meet with my teachers this year.

Fat chance.

Sammy sits down on the step. He's quiet. Just keeping me company.

Chapter Seven

I'm sitting on the floor in Nick's bedroom, studying for my history test while he lies on his bed. Sometimes it seems like he's thinking, staring at the ceiling. Other times he's staring at the ceiling but maybe not thinking so much. Nick turns on his side, facing the wall.

I feel badly for him, because I know he's really down. It's been almost a month since Nick got hurt. His body is healing, slowly, but his mental state stinks. But I'm also angry. Where's that resilience that Mom said he'd have?

Nick's getting around okay on his crutches at school, but he can't drive, and that stinks. His teammates include him in stuff, telling him stories about what Coach did at practice or some prank they pulled on a visiting team, but he wants to be playing ball, not listening to stories. Even the girls are still hanging on his every word, carrying his backpack and escorting him to class in the staff elevator. But none of it seems to make any difference. Nick is just sad.

My test is on the American Revolution. There are so many different "Acts"—the Tea Act, the Whiskey Act,

Townshend Act, the Revenue Act—and somehow I'm supposed to keep straight which tax is which and the dates, and it's all pretty much a scramble in my mind. I figure maybe it would do Nick some good to help me study.

"Can you tell me about the Federalists?"

"No," he says. And the way he says it, he's had enough of me.

I get off the floor and plunk myself down on Nick's bed, lying head to toe like Mom used to make us do when we'd go somewhere and we had to share a bed. The smell of his socks near my face brings me back to the last time we slept like this.

"Do you remember that vacation we went on with Mom to the Adirondacks when I was in sixth grade?" I ask.

"Yeah," Nick replies.

"There was that day that we went on the hike that we read about in the guidebook that Liza's mom lent us. In the book it said it was an easy hike 'for all levels.' Except when we got about a third of the way up, it got all rocky and steep, with those tree roots you had to climb over—and you and Mom were still going along fine, but I couldn't do it. It was just too hard."

Nick doesn't say anything, but I can feel that he's listening, trying to picture the story I'm telling.

"And then I sat down on a big rock, and told you just to leave me there, and pick me up on your way down. Do you remember what you said to me?"

"No," Nick says. But at least he's still with me.

"You said I could do it, just keep putting one foot in front of the other. And if you can't make it at any point, I'll carry you," I say, my voice cracking a little.

Nick sighs. "It's not the same, little sister. You can't carry me out of this one. But I know you would if you could." He turns all the way onto his stomach and puts the pillow over his head.

I don't know what else to say so I walk out, closing the door behind me.

I head to the kitchen, intent on shaking off Nick's gloom with an ice cream sandwich when I hear Mom talking on her cell. She's speaking quietly but she sounds pissed, her words coming fast and her voice higher than usual. I wonder who's on the other end, because Mom doesn't have a lot of friends she talks to on the phone or anywhere else. I mean I'm sure she hangs out with the other nurses and doctors at the hospital. But she doesn't have someone like Liza. And if she's dating, it's so on the down low that I've never been aware of it. Anyway, the other person is talking a lot louder than Mom, and now I can hear it's a man. I wonder if it's Mom's supervisor, George. And then I hear her say his name.

"I'm glad you found a job, Jeff, I really am, but I don't want your money after all this time... Yes, I know where McSweeney's is... no, are you crazy? I'm not coming over there now to talk this out in person … no, you can't come over here. Jeff—Nick is eighteen and your daughter is thirteen years old! That means you've been gone twelve years. You can't just waltz back into their lives…"

Mom is getting more agitated, and I know I'm eavesdropping, but I feel like I can't move. Does she talk to him sometimes, or did he just call her out of nowhere? I'm so freaked out that it takes me a minute to realize she didn't call me Layla or 'munk—just "your daughter." I've never really thought of myself as "his"—at least not in the way Mom said it—like, "your daughter, your responsibility." I'm not sure how it makes me feel.

Then Mom's walking toward the hallway, and for sure she'll lose it if she thinks I know she's been speaking to You-know-who. I quickly turn around and run as quietly as possible up the stairs and into my bedroom. I close the door behind me.

I sit down on my bed, heart racing, and Google "McSweeney's." It's a pub right in the middle of town, next to the old movie theater. Five minutes ago I didn't know the place existed but now I can see it in my mind's eye like I've been there a hundred times. Red brick exterior, green awning over the front door, letters spelling out the name in shiny brass. *I have to go.*

I text Liza.

"Ride your bike over here? I have something I need to do in town and I don't want to go alone."

"*K.*"

"*Won't take long,*" I text back. In fact, I have absolutely no idea how long it will take because I don't know what I'm planning to do. It's amazing to me that Liza trusts me and is on her way, without asking questions I can't answer.

Seven minutes later, she's in front of my house on her bike, helmet strapped snugly onto her head. I come out the front door and yell back over my shoulder, "Mom, be back in a little bit. I'm going for a ride with Liza." Mom never gives me any grief when I'm going anywhere with Liza. This time would be different if she knew.

I'm backing my bike out of the shed when I see Sammy riding down the street toward us. He's got his backpack on, like maybe he's coming from the library. I'm too jumpy to stand around talking, but he's already stopped where Liza is waiting for me, to say hi. Sammy and Liza are both very polite that way. Mom says they are well-bred, which always makes me think of dogs or horses.

Sammy turns toward me and says "Hi, Layla. Where you guys going?"

Liza is all ears too, because she's still in the dark.

"We're going on a stake out," I say.

"Who are we looking for?" Liza asks.

It seems like she has a right to know, so I say, "My dad."

"What?" they both ask in unison. I'm not sure how much Sammy knows about my personal life. I certainly haven't said a whole lot. But I guess being the "across the street neighbor" means that he at least knows my dad doesn't live with us. I'm sure through the grapevine he knows plenty more.

I decide to forge ahead; there doesn't seem to be much point in throwing in the towel now.

"Yeah. Apparently he's working in town. I just want to take a ride by." And I hop on my bike and start to pedal, figuring that will end the conversation.

But there is Sammy, right by my side. "Can I come?" he asks.

I'm about to say no when Liza says, "That's a good idea, Layla. It's good to have a boy with us. It's going to get dark soon."

I'm not sure how Sammy would protect us if we had a problem, but it's kind of sweet that he wants to help. It could just be that he's nosy, but it doesn't feel that way.

"Whatever," I say, but I'm glad.

We ride into the center of town—there's hardly anything open even though it's only six in the evening, just the big chain store pharmacy, Scoops—the ice cream shop, a couple of restaurants. The streets are empty. The other businesses—hair salons, clothing stores, two banks—are all closed. The movie theater only operates on the weekends, so it's dark too, but McSweeney's, the one bar on the main street, is all lit up.

We pull into the empty parking lot of the Post Office across the street. Now that I'm here, I feel scared and stupid. I'd like to turn around and ride home, get that ice cream sandwich from the kitchen that I never managed to grab and forget this whole escapade. But Liza and Sammy are looking at me expectantly, like we're on an adventure.

"What's your plan?" Liza asks. Liza likes to have a plan; she doesn't wing much.

"I don't think you can go in there," Sammy says. "You're underage."

He's trying to be helpful, but he's so serious that I have to smile. And then I feel a little braver.

Before I get any further in my thinking, the front door of McSweeney's opens. A young couple comes out, leaning in toward each other and laughing as the guy helps the girl put on her jacket. I'm watching them walk down the block and I don't notice the man who has come out a few steps behind them. But Sammy sees, and he touches my elbow and tilts his head in the man's direction.

He's a little bit like he is in my recurring dream. He's tall and his hair is kind of long, and he's handsome enough to explain why Mom didn't listen to reason when she ran off with him. But he doesn't look like me at all. He's Nick all the way, but twenty years older, long legs and soft blond curls and shoulders you want to lean into and cry on. I watch him as he cups his hand around his lighter and takes a drag from his cigarette. He's taking his time, maybe on a break. He looks like he's got a lot on his mind, the way he keeps staring into space and tapping his foot on the sidewalk. He looks lost.

"Are you going to talk to him? I could go with you," Liza offers.

"I could come too," Sammy says.

"No, I need to do this by myself." I have no idea what I'm going to say, but I feel like it's now or never. I pull off my bike helmet and hand it to Sammy, and smooth my hair. Liza pats me on the back, and I give her a thumbs-up and take a couple of steps forward.

Then I watch as my dad drops his cigarette to the ground and stamps it out with his foot. He looks up and down the street like maybe he had been expecting someone, and then he shrugs slightly and walks back into the pub.

I take my helmet back from Sammy, but I don't look at him or Liza.

"Let's get out of here. There's ice cream at my house," I say, and get back on my bike.

At least I know it's him and where he is. I'll figure out another way to reach him. I won't let this stop me. I can't.

Chapter Eight

McCarthy is walking back and forth in front of the classroom, clapping his hands and whining "C'mon guys." Tuesday of Thanksgiving week, and nobody can focus. Twenty-two kids who are already eating turkey and watching football in their heads.

I feel bad for McCarthy until he manages to get two words to float over the noise—"poetry unit." Now, what was a basically harmless hum has turned into a dangerous buzz, like the class might swarm and take McCarthy down. There's nothing worse than the annual "poetry unit." Even Liza, who likes all her subjects and gets good grades in everything, groans.

"Poetry? Right before vacation?" she says. "How can you do that to us?"

McCarthy stops pacing and sits down on the edge of his desk. He looks relieved that the class has quieted, waiting to hear how he'll react to Liza.

"Actually, I'm doing you all a favor," he says. "We only have one more day of school this week, so we're going to do the abbreviated version." McCarthy sounds reasonable, and we're all listening.

"And, not only is the unit super short, I'm switching it up," he continues.

"Is this a trick?" Callie says from the back row. She's put away her cell and is mostly paying attention, but she's on guard for any funny stuff McCarthy may try to pull.

"No, Callie, it's not a trick. Here's the deal. Each of you is going to be responsible for just one poem."

Kyle, who sits next to Callie and follows her around like a lovesick puppy, makes an unhappy face and snorts. He's handsome and popular, but he gets even worse grades than I do.

"Yes, Kyle, you will have to read the poem. The assignment is to write one paragraph explaining the poem, and a second paragraph answering this question: does the poem speak to you?" McCarthy says.

"I don't get what you mean about the second paragraph," Sammy says.

McCarthy smiles at Sammy, who can always be trusted to ask a relevant question at the right moment. If he weren't such a nice kid, everyone would hate him.

"Well, I mean a few different things. You can write about whether you like the poem or not. Or you can write about whether the poem has some special meaning to you. Or you can write about how you feel about the language of the poem or the music of the poem."

"Same old, same old," Kyle says to Callie, but just loud enough for everyone to hear. I have to agree. There's nothing really different about this than the usual poetry unit assignment: pick a poem, explain it, tell why you picked it. Even McCarthy is frowning a little, like he knows he's let us down. Except then he starts up again.

"Okay, so here's the kicker. You don't get to choose the poem you write about. I've chosen a different poem for each one of you."

McCarthy leaps up from his desk, looking comfortable and in control for the first time all period.

"I've tried to pick a poem I think will mean something to each of you. Kyle's poem is just for Kyle, and Liza's poem is just for Liza. I did the best I could based on what I've learned about your personalities and what you care about. So part of your essay should tell me if I got it right or not."

"That's pretty cool, Mr. McCarthy," I say, and then I clap my hand over my mouth because I can't believe that I actually said out loud what I was thinking. But it does seem kind of above and beyond that he took the time to consider each of us, and select twenty-two separate poems. No one has ever chosen a poem for me before.

'Thanks, Layla," he says, and then he walks up and down the aisles and hands out the poems, like he's giving each of us a gift.

"I think it's kind of creepy, Mr. M.," Callie says.

McCarthy sighs. "Not creepy, Callie—thoughtful."

But maybe Callie is right, like McCarthy is somehow fishing for personal info on us. I regret I said it was cool. I feel like I fell into a trap.

McCarthy gets to me, and hands me my poem, "The Road Not Taken" by Robert Frost. It isn't very long, maybe twenty lines, and there's a nice charcoal drawing of a forest and two paths going in different directions: one looks clear, like my front lawn after Mom makes Nick and me rake up and bag the leaves, and the other is kind of a mess. The sketch is really pretty, and I wonder—did McCarthy choose the sketch just for me too?

We spend the rest of the period learning about how poetry evolved from songs that the poets would recite before most people could read, and how it slowly developed into its own art form. We talk about different genres of poetry. Basically, McCarthy squeezes a two-week poetry unit into forty-two minutes. It's pretty impressive.

"Okay—the rest is up to you. No later than nine, people, to hand in your paragraphs. Don't make me stay up all night reading," McCarthy says above the chatter of kids showing each other their poems. I don't show mine to anyone; it seems like something private between me, McCarthy, and Robert Frost. The buzzer rings and I put the paper in my backpack, careful not to fold it so I don't ruin the picture. I feel silly, but I haven't looked forward to reading something this way in a long time, maybe since the last Harry Potter came out. And with how slowly I read, that book took me about a million years. I'm grateful that McCarthy picked something short.

I do my math and Earth Science homework, sitting in my usual spot on Nick's bedroom floor so I can keep an eye on him. He seems better and worse, if that's possible.

"What are you working on?" I ask. Nick is sitting at his desk typing on his laptop, and it's a relief to see him upright instead of sprawled on his bed.

He keeps at it, doesn't answer me. I look to see if maybe he's got his ear buds in and can't hear me, but he doesn't. I feel like crying. I could handle if Nick was mad at me, or even ignoring me. But it isn't like that. It's more like he's so far away inside himself that I don't even exist.

I pick up my notebooks and go to my room. No way I'm reading my personal poem in front of Nick.

I lie down on my bed and pull out the Xeroxed sheet of paper. I'm a little nervous I won't understand the poem, so I focus on the drawing again. Then I read the poem five times, maybe six, making sure I really get what Robert Frost is saying about these two paths. It's short enough that even with the somersaults the words do the first couple of times through, I get a handle on it pretty fast.

And then I ask myself the question.

Yes. The poem speaks to me, McCarthy. *It does.* Then I spend an hour writing about four lines trying to explain why.

In class the next morning, everyone is taking their time to get to their seats and talking about their plans for the days off. I'm still thinking about my poem, picturing those two paths again, when Sammy sits down and taps my foot with his, startling me.

"You guys home for Thanksgiving?"

"Where else would we be?" I ask, not really getting the question.

"I don't know," Sammy responds. "Sometimes we go to my grandparents', or my Aunt Pat's. But we're staying home this year. Maybe I'll see you around?"

"Maybe," I answer. It sounds nice, and I'm thinking about how that would happen when McCarthy starts talking.

"I hope you have an appreciation, now that you've come to own your own poem, of how exciting and meaningful poetry can be. It makes me sad that even educated people in our society write off poetry as something elitist."

A few of the kids look like they've actually heard McCarthy—maybe something about their poems spoke to them too. Liza was happy because McCarthy gave her a Shakespeare sonnet and, although it was really hard, she was able to figure it out, and it meant that McCarthy knew she could. And Sammy got the poem "Casey At The Bat," which was old and long but about baseball and Sammy loves baseball more than anything.

"Before I hand back the essays, I'm going to read from one, anonymously. This poem spoke forcefully to this student, as I hoped it would, and I believe the message applies to all of you. The poem is Robert Frost's The Road Not Taken."

And then McCarthy is holding my paper out in front of him, carefully obscuring the name at the top. I can feel my head tingling and I can barely hear what he is saying because the sound of my heart beating is so loud in my ears. My face is hot and I am sure that I have gone lobster red. All I can do is stare down at my hands in my lap and sit perfectly still so I don't implode. He reads the poem first, and then continues.

"This is what your classmate wrote:

'In the poem, the narrator is deciding whether to follow a path that's already been carved out by others, or to do something new. I think Frost's point is that there's nothing wrong about either decision, but you should be aware that you're making a choice, and it might be better to do something original.

'This poem speaks to me because I'm also facing a choice in my life. I can keep going down the path I'm on, but it feels like a dead end. Or I can choose to do something totally different—even though I don't know where it leads yet. It's my choice whether to break free. It could be scary, but it also could be big. I hope I have the courage to choose the new path.'"

McCarthy finishes and a couple of the jokers in the class start to clap, but then Liza and Sammy and McCarthy join in for real, and the other kids aren't sure what to do, so they clap too. And then I realize that I'm the only one not clapping, so anyone who hadn't noticed my mortified face before now knows that it's my paper. I'm nauseous and pumped at the same time; no one has ever applauded any academic effort of mine, not even Mom, not even in private.

"Okay, that's enough now," McCarthy says. Then he shuffles my paper in with the others on the pretense that I'm still anonymous, and hands out the papers. When he gives me back mine, I think he winks but I can't swear it. I smile a tiny smile, which grows when I see the grade, A. It's the best grade I've gotten all semester in any of my classes. It may even be worth the embarrassment.

After class, I walk to my locker to switch out my notebooks for Earth Science. I'm still holding my paper against my chest, afraid if I let it go it won't be real. Then

I hear Callie and Kyle talking at Callie's locker, across the hallway from mine.

"I can't believe McCarthy read her paper out loud. I mean, it's amazing that she wrote something that made any sense at all. Usually her papers are crap like yours," Callie says.

"Shut up," Kyle says. "Probably McCarthy's hot for her."

"You're a pig, Kyle," Callie says, and shoves him playfully away from her locker in the direction of their next class.

"Well, men are pigs," Kyle says.

"I think McCarthy just felt bad for her," Callie says, "so he figured he'd make a big deal of her stupid paper so she'd feel better about herself."

I scrunch up my essay into a ball and throw it on top of the pile in my locker.

Chapter Nine

On Thanksgiving, the cars arrive at Sammy's house at just after three, pulling into his driveway or parking in front, spilling out relatives. Not a ton of people, maybe fifteen or so—an older couple who must be his grandparents, aunts and uncles, a whole mess of cousins. Most of the adults are carrying casseroles, one woman has a pie. And the kids all have balls—footballs or basketballs or soccer balls. I even spot a golf ball. One little girl is holding a reindeer stuffed animal that's almost as big as she is, like she's already moved on to Christmas, which is a little off, since Sammy's family is Jewish. Whatever. I wonder if any of them notice me sitting on my couch in my living room across the street, watching through the picture window.

Mom's been in the kitchen most of the day. She managed to get Thanksgiving off from the hospital, although now she'll have to work the rest of the long weekend. I think she really wanted to be here for Nick, to cheer him up. Mom's kind of a tyrant in the kitchen when she actually has the opportunity and the time to have the place to herself, so I'm staying out of her way. She's making all the stuff Nick likes—which is resulting in a tremendous amount of food for three people, and a pretty weird combination of traditional turkey and fixings, right along with baked ziti and fried eggplant marinara. At this point, if Italian food is what gets Nick to sit at the table with us and maybe have a laugh or two, it's fine by me.

I'm still daydreaming about Sammy's traditional Thanksgiving with all that family, and maybe even a little bit about Sammy, when the doorbell rings. I jump out of my chair so fast that I trip over my own feet and go lurching toward the hallway.

"Who could that be?" Mom yells out from the kitchen. She's concentrating on trimming brussel sprouts that only she will eat.

When I get to the door, I feel a surge of nerves that starts in the pit of my stomach and travels all the way to my ears. What have I done? But it's too late to go back now.

I open the door and he's standing there. He's not super dressed up, wearing jeans and button-down shirt, but it's ironed, and a sports jacket. His hair is damp and on his cheek there's a little cut covered by a band-aid where he must have messed up shaving. He's holding a bouquet of red and yellow and orange flowers—the "autumn special" at the grocery story is my guess. Still, I think it is nice that he's made the effort.

For a second, I think that I'm back in that dream I have where my dad comes to the house and fixes all my problems–the one that always ends with me I waking up feeling sick with disappointment. But I know this isn't a dream because I *made* this happen. And I don't feel sad–I feel hopeful. I know my father can't fix everything, but maybe I've made a start by bringing us all together for the holiday.

"You must be Layla," he says.

"I'm surprised you remember her name." Mom came up behind me so quietly I didn't even hear her. She's wearing an apron stained with tomato sauce tied around her waist and her purple crocs that she wears at the hospital when she has to be on her feet for long stretches. I wonder if she's self-conscious, but then she steps in front of me so she's facing Jeff, in between us like she's afraid he's going to hurt me.

"I gave her that name," Jeff says.

"And that was the last contribution you made." I've never seen Mom so fierce. I'm no expert on chemistry, but there's an energy between them. It's like when you put the popcorn in the microwave and there's that minute before it gets going, and then it's all out crazy, until you leave it a few seconds too long and it's a burnt mess that you have to throw away.

They're still facing off silently at the front door when Nick comes slowly down the stairs. He must have heard the doorbell ring. Maybe he thought it was one of his friends, but the truth is, he's isolated himself so much the last couple of weeks that hardly anyone stops by looking for him these days.

When Nick finally reaches the bottom landing, he looks squarely at Jeff, who nods at him once. Nick balls up his fists at his sides but says nothing. He turns around, and slowly goes back up the stairs, slamming the door to his bedroom so hard the walls rattle.

"Why does he walk that way?" Jeff asks.

"It's not permanent," I say quickly, because maybe Jeff is worried. "He hurt himself playing basketball but he's getting better and—"

"What are you doing here? I told you not to come around," Mom says.

Jeff locks eyes with Mom but tilts his head toward me.

"Layla invited me," he says. "She dropped off a note at McSweeney's." He tries to hand me the flowers, but Mom intercepts him, shoving them back into his hands.

"Layla is a child," Mom says.

"My child," Jeff says quietly. He looks down at his shoes, and I notice he's tapping his foot nervously. I wonder if he's been doing that the whole time.

"I think you gave up your right to say that twelve years ago," Mom says. But now she doesn't sound angry so much as sad. I don't know why, but it occurs to me that if the two of them had been married back when they had me and Nick, maybe Jeff would have been different, more committed. But as it is, he's just a guy who didn't know how to be part of a family.

After a minute or two, Jeff asks, "Are you going to invite me in?"

Mom fidgets with her ponytail, taking out the elastic and gathering her hair up and tying it back again, something we both do when we're nervous or stalling for time. I give her my best "please, Mom," look, but I don't say anything. Then she shakes her head slowly.

"I don't think that would be a good idea."

Jeff opens his mouth to protest, but then shuts it, as though he's thought better of it. "Okay, then," he says. "Thanks for trying, Layla. It's great to see how you're turning out. You're beautiful, just like your name."

For a second, I think we might hug, but it would be embarrassing if we tried and Mom stopped us. So I stick out my hand in what I hope is a business-like manner, and his hand feels cool and smooth in a way I wasn't expecting. Mom watches silently as we shake hands, and when we finish, Jeff turns and walks out the door. Mom closes it slowly but firmly behind him, and locks it for good measure. I wonder what Jeff thought when he heard the click of the deadbolt.

Mom walks back into the kitchen without looking at me, but as she passes the stairs she yells up to Nick, "He's gone, Honey." I resist the urge to run up to Nick's room and find out what he's thinking, because he's probably pissed off at me if he's figured out I was the one who asked Jeff here. I'm feeling confused and lonely as I follow Mom into the kitchen.

I sit down at the kitchen table and start talking fast, before I lose my nerve.

"I can't believe you're going to let him have Thanksgiving dinner at McSweeney's." For some reason I picture Jeff as a bartender, suavely mixing complicated drinks and doling out sage advice to the customers, but for all I know he's washing dishes or waiting tables. "It's a family holiday."

Mom sighs. "Oh, 'munk. It's so much more complicated than you can understand," she says.

"You can't tell me what to think about him." Although I have no idea what I think about him.

Mom puts down the peeler she was using on the sweet potatoes, wipes her hands on her apron, and sits next to me at the table.

"No, I can't. I can only tell you what I think about him, what I know about him, as a man and as a father. He's irresponsible and immature. A drifter." Mom softens her voice, and moves to the chair next to me, putting her arm around my shoulders.

"Can't people change?" I really need to know.

"Some can, and some just are who they are. I don't believe he's changed. He's not a bad person, or I wouldn't have loved him. And he helped bring two amazing people into the world. But actions have consequences, 'munk, and his leaving means he gave up having a part in our lives. When you're older, you can make some other choice for yourself if you want."

"So am I just supposed to pretend he's not in town? He must have come back here, of all the places in the world, for a reason, and maybe we're that reason." I lean my head on Mom's shoulder, as she strokes my hair. I could kick myself for my weakness.

"I can't sit by and watch him hurt you, Sweetie. And that's what would happen. He'd get involved with you, and then when it didn't suit him anymore, he'd be gone. That's who he is."

We sit like this for a few more minutes, until Mom says she needs to finish cooking if we're going to eat dinner while it's still Thanksgiving. I help her, pouring the cranberry sauce into a bowl, adding the Parmesan cheese to the top of the ziti. When the turkey is ready, Mom goes at it with the electric knife, carving efficiently but angrily. I wonder if she's picturing my dad.

"Nick, come down for dinner," Mom calls from the bottom of the stairs. I hold my breath, waiting to see if he'll emerge from his room. When he does, I kind of wish he hadn't.

"That was quite a stunt you pulled there, little Sis," he says. His voice sounds choked, like it's struggling to get through his throat. "You might have consulted with me first," he says, so quietly that Mom doesn't even turn around from the stove where she's warming up the gravy.

"You know, Nick, it's not exactly like you've been here for me lately."

But he's probably right. I messed up on this one. Another failure.

After we eat as much as three people possibly can, I clear the table. Mom goes to bed almost immediately, because she has to be at the hospital early. Nick sweeps up the floor and loads the dishwasher, shakes out the crumbs on the tablecloth.

"You okay?" he asks, after the kitchen is restored to its usual tidy state.

"I guess," I respond, wrapping up the ziti.

"You know, I never would have done what you did. But I get it. There's always that crazy fantasy that they'll get back together, and we'll be one big happy family," Nick says. He stops drying the platters and looks at me. "I hope, for your sake, you're over that now."

Nick climbs slowly up the stairs to his room, and without even seeing or hearing the music, I know he's back in one of his video game fantasies, headed off someplace where unhappiness and conflict and dashed hopes only exist virtually and not in reality. I almost wish I could go with him. Instead, I go out to the front porch and sink into the swing, rocking myself gently. It's soothing, and the crisp air clears my head a little.

It's only 8:00 p.m., but the visiting cars at Sammy's house are all gone. The house is still lit up, even the bedrooms upstairs, and I picture his family reviewing the day, laughing about pranks the kids pulled this year, and talking about the delicious food. Then I see Sammy come out the side door, taking out the trash.

"Hey," I shout.

It takes him a second to locate where the sound is coming from, but when he sees it's me, a big smile breaks across his face.

"Hey! Can I come over?"

"Sure," I say, and then wonder if this is a good idea, given how the rest of my day has gone.

Sammy finishes tying up the cans of the garbage pails with bungee cords to prevent the raccoons from getting in and making a mess, and then he jogs over. He bounds up the stairs, and I realize he's gotten taller again.

He sits down on the swing with me. "How was Thanksgiving?" he asks.

"Pretty weird," I say. I take a deep breath, and decide to fill him in. I mean, he went on the reconnaissance mission; it sort of seems like he earned this.

"I invited my dad, and then my mom didn't let him in the house," I say. That pretty much sums it up.

"Wow," Sammy responds.

"Yeah. I feel so stupid. About everything."

Sammy leans forward, his elbows on his knees, and looks at me, slowing the swing until I have to look up at him.

"I think you're amazing, Layla."

"Why? For ruining everyone's holiday?"

"For trying, for taking a chance. Just like you wrote about with your poem—even though you didn't know how it would turn out, you did the thing that no one else had the nerve to do." Sammy sounds so convinced that I almost think he's right. But then I remember the looks on their faces—Mom, Jeff, and Nick—and I know there's no way to see this as a good thing.

I shake my head, and the tears I have been holding back start to flow.

"Hey, don't cry," Sammy says. He puts his arm around me and starts the swing rocking again.

Chapter Ten

When my alarm rings, I keep my eyes closed for a few seconds so that my ears can work better. Total silence. Nick is probably halfway to school already. It's amazing that he gets up in the morning when he stays up so late gaming. I imagine Mom, just off her shift, changing into normal shoes and splashing her face with cold water, rummaging in her bag for her keys so she can come home and sleep. But she won't get much rest today—parent-teacher conferences are at three. Not sure who I feel worse for—Mom or me.

I take a long time getting ready, making sure my clothes are just right, my hair neatly pulled back. As if looking what Mom calls "well groomed" today will make a difference in what the teachers say to her. I know it's stupid. I also know that Mom's learned not to expect a lot. She's not surprised or even all that disappointed anymore when the best my teachers can report is that I try hard and I'm well-behaved. Only poor misguided McCarthy might stretch to say something good.

I pass Nick's closed bedroom door and I can't resist peeking inside. If you didn't know him like I do, you'd think he was back to his old pre-injury self. He's been doing his schoolwork, hanging out with his friends on the weekends. He can't play ball—he won't this year, and likely won't play in college now either. But he's been going to practice and the games, to chill with the team. Still—it's like a little piece of him has died—the part that would fight for himself. And fight for me.

I open his door and I'm hit with a blast of cold air. The windows are wide open even though it can't be more than twenty degrees outside. It's Nick's not so subtle attempt to freshen up the place, the smell of teenage boy and the cigarette he sneaks when he's super down, lingering in the air. You have to admire his effort. But he's hiding something deeper than the incriminating odor—a desperate combination of frustration and hopelessness and disappointment. Nick's room reeks of it, and the feelings are contagious. I'm no narc about this stuff, but maybe Nick would see how much he has going for him if he weren't so zoned out a good chunk of his waking hours. I spot his signature red lighter on his desk, and I take it, stuffing it in the front pocket of my jeans. It's a useless gesture. He probably has a couple more in here somewhere. But at least I feel like I've done something.

I get through my morning classes, flying even further under the radar than usual. I know the better strategy would be to raise my hand and answer every question in a last-ditch effort to impress the teachers before they sit down with Mom, but I just can't get myself to do it. When I walk into the cafeteria during lunch, Liza motions me over to where she and Sammy have saved me a seat. It's not their fault, but their cheerful faces irritate me, and I take a few steps in the opposite direction. Then I roll my eyes and turn back, walking slowly to their table.

"What's up with you?" Liza asks. "You're acting weird." There's no putting anything past Liza. I can see Sammy open his mouth like he's going to come to my defense, but I put my fingers lightly on the top of his hand where it's resting on the table, and shake my head.

"She's right," I say. "But I don't want to talk about it. It doesn't matter." We eat our sandwiches in silence, my stomach twisting with nerves so that I can barely get my pb&j down. I put my hand in my pocket and feel the reassuring cool, smooth surface of Nick's lighter. It calms me a little, and I'm able to think.

It isn't that I'm jealous of Liza and Sammy and how proud they make their parents. I mean it *is* that, but it's also more than that. There's this huge disconnect between who I know I am deep down, and the girl everyone sees. As if there's this really smart kid inside me, trapped, desperate to get out and prove herself to the world. But the Layla people know is a lousy student, trudging along, reading at a snail's pace and always behind, writing words that get all mangled before they even hit the page. It's just so unfair.

L ast period. Earth Science. We do kind of an interesting lab experiment about vinegar and baking soda and putting out flames. But my head just isn't in it. The bell rings and everyone starts talking, drowning out Miss Cranston as she tries to give a last-minute homework assignment. Only Liza seems able to make out the teacher's words through the noise, as she dutifully writes down page numbers on her planner.

"Coming to the bus?" Sammy asks me.

"In a minute. I have to get my math notebook from my locker," I say. "You go out with Liza."

"I'd rather go out with you," he says quietly; that sweet, slightly mischievous smile on his face again. I can't for the life of me figure out why he likes me better than Liza, but it does make me happy.

"Go on," I say. I suddenly wish he would put his arm around me again like he did on the porch on Thanksgiving, but that's not going to happen here. I turn and walk out of the classroom.

I head to my locker on the third floor, where a bunch of kids are working their combinations and frantically grabbing folders and textbooks so they don't miss their busses or carpools. I watch them scurrying around like diligent little mice, and picture them running on wheels in their cages until they collapse. So pointless.

In a few minutes, the frenzy of activity in the hallway clears. There are teachers all over the building preparing for parents to arrive, but the only classroom near my locker is woodshop, and no parent ever meets with Mrs. Perlmutter. What would she say? Your child sands and stains very well? It's a safe bet she snuck out before the last bell rang, grateful that she doesn't have to stick around for a lot of meaningless interactions. Woodshop is my strongest subject, but even I don't ask Mom to meet with Perlmutter.

I open my locker. The pile of tests and papers has grown, bad grade layered on top of bad grade, until it's almost a third of the way up the walls, reaching my magazine photos of Maroon Five and Taylor Swift. I can see the individual grades poking out—mostly Cs and C-pluses, a couple of B-minuses, and my lone A from McCarthy on the poetry assignment. A tower of underachievement. For a few seconds I stare at the papers, as though by sheer force of will, I can transform the grades into As—grades like Nick gets, barely trying—assignments that my mom would pin up on the refrigerator and would make her smile each time she passed by on her way to the kitchen table.

But that's never going to happen. It doesn't matter how hard I try or how many hours I spend on my assignments, I can never make Mom proud. Everything I do just seems to make her sigh, put her arm around me, and give me this pitying look that says, "*it's okay, Layla, I know you can't do any better. This is who you are.*" Even when I tried to invite Jeff for dinner, it was a total fail. I couldn't pull off my plan to bring the four of us together for one lousy meal. I got an "F" for Thanksgiving.

As I look at the pile of papers again I have a vision of my mom going from classroom to classroom to meet with each of my teachers. At the beginning of every conference, Mom sits up straight in the chair across from the teacher's desk and plasters a big hopeful smile on her face, introduces herself, maybe shakes hands. And each time, the teacher starts with something positive–the principal must tell them they have to do that–"Layla is always on time to class," one says, or "Layla is kind to the other students," and then the let down follows. Mom's smile fades and her shoulders sag as each teacher goes over my work and tells her about my bad grades and my poor prospects for success. Imagining the scene, I feel the sting of tears forming in my eyes.

"Bet you're looking forward to your mom coming for conferences as much as I am," Kyle sniggers. Like he's read my mind. I hadn't noticed him at his locker, but he breaks the spell I was in.

"I hardly think it's the same," I mutter under my breath, because Kyle has the IQ of a caveman, and the personality to match. I don't say anything else because

I'm afraid my voice may catch and he'll hear that I was almost crying. I turn my body completely toward my locker and away from Kyle and wipe one stray tear with the sleeve of my sweatshirt.

Kyle finishes whatever he was doing and slams the locker shut. "Later, loser," he says. He's pissed me off and I'm about to fling back some clever response when I realize that I'm less annoyed at Kyle and more upset at the thought of all of my teachers ratting me out to Mom. It's just so unfair. If only I could think of some way out of this.

My hands are shaking and I don't know if it's anger or frustration or some emotion unique to me that doesn't have a name. All I know is that I want this feeling to go away–I need to *do* something to change this afternoon so that Mom won't find out I'm a loser, just like Kyle said.

I jam my hands into the pockets of my jeans to keep them still. My fingers close around Nick's lighter and I pull it out, turning it over in my palm. It feels cool and smooth. I took it from Nick's room without a plan, but now it feels like the answer I've been looking for. It's so easy—so clean. Not a permanent solution. Not a solution at all when I really think about it, but I push that out of my head. It will work for today. There will be no tests or essays for Mom to review with my teachers. No hopeful smiles that fade to disappointment. I won't have to deal with her well-meaning but unconvincing attempts to cover her feelings, or her lame encouragement. I can make it so today will just be a blank, like this semester never happened. It's in my hands.

I get down on one knee and flick open the lighter. The flame dances—it looks happy, eager. I touch it to the corner of the bottom of the pile—the first math test of the semester, a weak 72. I watch as the fractions and square roots—xs and ys—ignite, passing the torch to Social Studies and the Boston Tea Party—a puny 74. The flames eat each subject and grade, spiraling upward and gaining speed, carrying the destruction to the next, in a satisfying pyre. I feel a wave of relief as I watch all my wasted efforts disappear.

It doesn't take long for the fire to make its way through my assignments. But then tongues of flame rise to singe the bottom of my winter jacket, licking up the walls of my locker and incinerating the taped-up photos and newspaper clippings, and all the stuff I've so carefully added since sixth grade. Instead of the fire dying down after it erased the evidence of my bad school work—like I had pictured in my rush to figure a way out of these conferences—it grows like it's just gotten going. I wonder whether I can tamp out the flames with my foot and stick my sneaker in tentatively, but it's too hot and the fire is too big. *Oh my God, what have I done?* I slam the door of the locker shut, Ms. Cranston's voice in my head droning on that cutting off the oxygen will extinguish the flames.

But Ms. Cranston and I haven't figured in the other factors here, like the ventilation slits on the top of my locker, letting in plenty of oxygen. Or the side walls of these old lockers that don't meet the back wall all the way, leaving a thin crack for the flames to go from my locker to Liza's, and then to the other four lockers in the row. Which is exactly what's happening.

I watch, paralyzed, as smoke starts to come out of the vents at the top of the lockers. I don't move until the fire alarm sounds and I feel the first spray of water from the overhead sprinklers hit the top of my head.

I bolt, tossing Nick's lighter in the garbage can outside the girls' bathroom.

When I get outside, the buses have already left. I sink down next to the flagpole and watch as the fire engines arrive. The teachers and a handful of kids that were still hanging around spill out of the doors. It isn't the neat formation we have during fire drills; more like the building is spitting out its unwanted contents before it goes up in smoke. But can it really be that bad? I mean, whatever's in those few lockers is toast, but I think that's it. For the first time I wish to God that I didn't have the locker next to Liza. She doesn't deserve this.

And then, like I've conjured her, Liza is standing there, looking down at me where I'm sitting on the ground.

"Hey," Liza says. "You look like crap. And where's your jacket?"

And then I start to bawl like a baby, soot mixing with the tears as they streak down my face.

Liza sits next to me and puts her arm around my shoulders.

Chapter Eleven

When the all-clear sounds twenty minutes later, Liza stands up and holds out her hand and pulls me to my feet. I wipe my eyes and take a deep breath. She hasn't asked why I'm crying, and I haven't volunteered anything. Maybe she figures it's whatever was bugging me at lunch.

"Come on," Liza says. "I'll call my mom to pick us up."

I grab her wrist, almost making her drop her cell.

"Please, don't. I can't go home yet. Please, let's walk."

"It's almost a mile to your house and it's freezing, Layla."

While we're standing there, the fire engines pull out of the school's driveway. A young firefighter with thick, black hair and a dazzling smile leans out the passenger window and salutes us. Liza gamely waves back.

"I love firemen," she says, dreamily. "Heroes, but they can also cook."

When Liza turns back to look at me, all I can do is shake my head.

"Okay, okay," she says, "we'll walk." Liza unzips her jacket and pulls off her sweatshirt, hands it to me, and then puts her jacket back on. It doesn't help much in this weather, and I'm still wet from when the sprinklers went off, but it's warm from her body and comforting.

We leave the school grounds and head down Cedar Street, Liza chatting non-stop. I can't process what she's saying, but I get from her tone that she has no idea why the Fire Department was there or that she's at all affected. For a second, I think about just letting her go on that way. But I can't.

"Liza—you don't know what I've done."

"What are you talking about?" she asks.

I stop walking, and after step or two, Liza stops too and turns back toward me. I take a deep breath and do my best to look her in the eye, but it's too hard. I look down at my feet.

"I set fire to the papers in my locker so my mom wouldn't be able to have parent-teacher conferences today." I say it so fast and so quietly that Liza makes me repeat myself.

"And then the fire spread from my locker to yours, all the way down the line."

Liza doesn't say a word. She turns her back on me and starts walking again, fast. I try to keep up, and I'm quickly out of breath. At first, I think she's going to break out into a run to get away from me, but half a block later I realize she's not. After another block, I risk a sideways glance at her. Her mouth is a thin line and she's staring straight ahead. Her hands are clenched into fists.

"Are you mad at me?" I ask.

"Well of course I'm mad at you!" Liza hardly ever raises her voice and it's shocking to hear her now. But if anyone ever deserved to be yelled at, it's me.

"You destroyed all my stuff! My binders and my class notes and my assignments—whatever's not in my backpack—was incinerated right along with yours!" Liza stops and throws her backpack down hard on the pavement, narrowly missing smashing her cell phone stowed in the front pocket. I've never seen her this angry. And I get it. Torching my crappy schoolwork is one thing; taking her stuff along for the ride is quite another.

"I'm so sorry, Liza. You have to believe that I never meant for that to happen."

"And what exactly did you think would happen when you set fire to the school?" Liza asks. She picks up her backpack, and throws it roughly over one shoulder.

I catch hold of the top of her arm and turn her toward me, forcing her to stop marching forward. She pulls away immediately, but something in her eyes softens.

"I just didn't want my mom to come today."

Liza starts walking again, but at a regular pace, slowly shaking her head. When she lets out a long exhale, she doesn't look so pissed off anymore.

"You realize that's crazy, right? Your teachers have records of your grades and copies of your assignments—they don't need the actual papers, Layla."

"I know, I know," I say. "I wasn't thinking straight. And I'm really, really sorry about your locker."

We walk the rest of the way to my house in silence.

Mom's car is in the driveway. I've been so consumed with trying to explain to Liza that I haven't figured out what I'm going to say to Mom. I've never really lied big to her. Plenty of omissions—like covering for Nick, or when I went to McSweeney's to look for Jeff—but not outright lies. I don't want to start now.

Mom opens the door before I can even get my key out of my pocket.

"Layla! I was worried about you. We got an email that there was a smoke condition at the school, and the conferences were all delayed an hour. But then you didn't come home—" and then she notices Liza, several feet behind me.

"Oh, hi, Liza. If I had known Layla was with you, I wouldn't have been concerned," Mom says. She reaches for her pocketbook, which is hanging on the back of a kitchen chair, and pulls out her keys.

"Okay, I have to go. Be good, girls. There's lasagna in the fridge," she says. She's almost out the door when she turns around.

"Layla, where's your jacket?"

"I left it in my locker when the fire alarm went off," I say, relieved to be telling the truth, for now.

When Mom leaves, I sink down onto the living room couch and hold my head in my hands.

"What am I going to do, Liza? When they figure out it was me, I'll be expelled for sure. I'm already at the bottom of the heap with my grades; who's going to care if I go down?"

Liza starts pacing the length of the living room. She always paces when she's deep in thought, so I do my best to keep quiet. I know there's no way out of this. But if there were a way, Liza would find it.

"Listen. That fire could have been set in any one of the six lockers and spread to the others. So there are six kids who could've done it. And right now, no one knows who struck the match."

"Lighter," I say, under my breath. "But so what? I can't blame it on someone else." My voice has gone high and squeaky, practically strangled in my throat. Could that really be what Liza is suggesting?

"Of course not," she says. "But if someone else came forward and took the blame, said it was an accident, then you'd be off the hook." Liza perches on the ottoman and puts her hands on my knees.

"Oh no, no…"

"Listen, Layla. I'll say I just came from science class, and I wanted to try out another theory of how to put out a fire, like we did in lab. I lit a match by my locker, and then I smothered it with… I don't know—like, nail polish remover. I didn't realize that it was flammable, and before I knew it…"

"Oh, Liza. You can't do this. You'll never pull it off!" I rush to the kitchen sink and retch, just a hint of peanut butter at the back of my throat.

"It will work, Layla," Liza says calmly. "No one would ever think that I'd set a fire intentionally. I don't even leave class to go to the bathroom unless it's a dire emergency. You're lucky I'm a goody-two-shoes. I'm going to save your butt."

"I don't know, Liz—" I stammer.

"Okay. Here's the thing. If I'm going to confess, I have to do it first thing in the morning. No way a person like me could sit on this any longer. So text me tonight and let me know. Give me my sweatshirt; I need to go."

When Mom comes home from the conferences I'm sitting in the kitchen, lazily moving lasagna around my plate. Nick breezed in half an hour ago and went up to his room without even saying hi. I still haven't decided what to do, and my head is pounding.

"'munk, don't you want to know what your teachers had to say?" Mom asks. She actually sounds cheerful, which is so weird.

"Not so much." I manage.

"Well, they all told me how hard you try, and what a good example you set for your classmates in terms of attitude and respectfulness. I was very proud. Those character traits are just as important as good grades," Mom says. I cringe.

"And your English teacher, Mr. McCarthy, is particularly impressed with you. Says you have a lot of potential."

When I don't respond, Mom seems to think she needs to fill the silence.

"You know, 'munk, some kids don't really blossom until high school."

I look away. Not sure how getting expelled from middle school would fit in with Mom's vision of my future.

"Can I be excused?" I say.

"You barely ate."

"I had a big lunch," I lie. I run up to my room and close the door. I pull out my phone.

"Okay. Let's do it."

Chapter Twelve

When I look at my cell, it's 2:36 a.m. I roll over and pull the blankets over my head, but when I check again, it's 2:39. There's no point in trying. I'm not sleeping.

I whip my blankets off. My whole body is burning with shame. It doesn't matter that Liza was the one who came up with this idea, because I'm going to let her hang. What kind of a person does that? And how will I ever make it up to her so she trusts me again? It will always be there between us. Even if Liza says she forgives me, which she will because that's the kind of person she is, our friendship won't ever be the same.

I get out of bed and walk quietly down the hall past Mom's room, forgetting for a moment that she's at work. I knock on Nick's door and he lets out a lazy grumble that I take for "come in." He looks so serene lying in his bed, not a care in the world. He's not a thrasher like I am, and his sheets and blankets are pulled taut over his long body.

When I climb into the bed next to him, he opens his eyes for a second and then squeezes them shut.

"What are you, five years old?" he asks. But his voice is kind, and I know we are sharing a memory from when we were little kids and I used to have nightmares and end up curled next to him.

"I'm scared," I say.

"It's just a bad dream, 'munk. It'll be better in the morning."

I wish that were true.

I don't remember falling asleep, but when I wake up in Nick's bed, he's already gone.

I brush my teeth until my gums bleed, and then I rinse so long with Mom's horrible mouthwash that tears come to my eyes. But I can't get rid of the taste. The taste of betrayal. I'm letting Liza take the blame for something I've done. I look in the mirror and I see a monster. I hate myself.

When I get to the bus stop, Sammy's already there, gently tossing a ball back and forth with a little kid from down the block. When he sees me, he raises his eyebrows up and down like in those old Groucho Marx movies, and then pretends like he's shooting an arrow at my heart.

"What's up, buttercup?" Sammy says.

"You're so weird." But he's made me smile for a second, and that's a big accomplishment.

We get on the bus—the same little one we've been taking since kindergarten. The benches are tight, and the ceiling is low—Sammy has to practically bend in half to get down the aisle without banging his head. We squeeze onto a seat together in the back, our bodies touching at the knee, elbow, and shoulder. I lean in a little.

"Still upset about your locker?" Sammy asks. For a second I think about telling him the truth. Would he understand how I could sell out Liza to save myself? I can't risk it.

"Kind of," I say.

"Did a lot of your stuff get ruined?"

"Yeah. But the only thing I really care about is my jacket." Telling the truth about something calms me a little.

"That was crazy, how that all went down. I wonder what happened," Sammy muses. "They'll figure it out sooner or later. The fire department has forensic guys for things like this—they can tell what started a fire, how it spread, everything. I saw it on a CSI episode."

I stare out the window.

I don't see Liza the first few periods of school, and I wonder whether she's decided not to go through with it. I wouldn't blame her—bailing would be the only rational thing to do. Each minute that goes by without her in school,

I become more convinced that she's stayed home, faking some illness, so she can avoid me and avoid our plan. So I actually gasp a little when I get to McCarthy's class and Liza is sitting in her seat, a brand new notebook in front of her, and a second copy of the book we've been reading, *The Perks of Being a Wallflower*, open on her desk.

I sit in my seat next to her. She doesn't turn toward me, but nods almost imperceptibly. I can't risk my voice, which I'm sure will give away my nerves, so I scribble a note on a piece of paper.

"Thanks so much, Liza. I'm so sorry." I slide it across to her, making sure McCarthy isn't watching.

Liza reads the note and looks up at me, and I see her eyes are red. Before I can say anything, she writes a note in her beautiful handwriting and passes it back to me.

"It's okay. The principal called my mother in. I hadn't figured on that. It was hard to lie. I'm not a liar."

The room is spinning and there's a whooshing sound in my ears that makes me feel like my head might explode. When it clears a little, I hear McCarthy. He's reading a passage from the book, and it's like he can see inside my head. "It was the look on her face when she said it. And how much she meant it. It suddenly made everything seem like it really was. I felt terrible. Just terrible."

My hand shoots up into the air before my brain has time to come up with a plan.

"Yes, Layla?" McCarthy says.

"I need to go. It's an emergency," I blurt out. I grab my backpack and head to the door. Kyle turns to Callie and stage whispers, "must be that time of the month," and most of the boys, and some of the girls, laugh. But the bell is going to ring any minute and the next period is lunch. McCarthy lets me go without asking any questions.

We're not allowed to leave school grounds during the day, but I figure I can't really get in any more trouble than I'm going to be in anyway. I run through the soccer field to avoid the security guard in front, and I don't stop until I reach the high school, half a mile away. It's an open campus, so no one even notices when I go in the front doors and head downstairs to the gym. If Nick isn't in class, he'll be here. He's still King of the Gym, hanging out with his teammates and with the girls who hang on them.

I'm breathing hard, and I hear Nick's friend Travis say, "Bro, your little sister's here and she's about to keel over."

Nick is sitting in the back row of the bleachers and I watch as he peels away from some redhead I've never seen before. He takes his time to get over to where I'm standing, like he doesn't really want to deal with me. When he finally gets close enough, he puts his hand firmly on my back and guides me over to the boys' locker room.

He ducks in for a second to make sure no one's inside before pulling me in and locking the door.

"What the heck are you doing here, 'munk?"

I tell him everything, hyperventilating so badly that at moments I can't speak.

When I'm done, Nick looks at me for what seems like a long time.

"That's really low, 'munk. Setting the fire was stupid, but how could you do that to your best friend?"

There's no answer. I hope by confessing to him, he'll understand that I need his help to make this right. I need the old Nick, the one who stayed calm and knew what to do when things were screwed up.

"Okay, let's go," he says, pulling his keys out of his pocket. I don't ask where. Sometimes you just have to trust.

Nick pulls into our driveway and kills the engine.

"Don't move," he says. *Where would I go?*

Fifteen minutes later, Mom is out of bed and dressed and we're on our way to school. Nick has debriefed her, sparing me. Mom buckles herself in the front seat, and flips the sun visor down so she can look at me in the mirror.

"Listen, 'munk. This is bad. All of it. The fire, the damage you caused, the scheme to have Liza take the blame—even if it was her idea, as Nick explained. But we're going to walk into that principal's office with our heads held high. You're a good kid. This doesn't change that."

I hope Principal Belzer sees it the same way.

We walk down the hallway, Mom on my right side with her arm loosely around my waist, and Nick on my left. He's so tall compared to the middle school kids that even the ones who don't recognize him from the basketball team stop and stare. I'm trying hard to keep my chin up, like Mom said, so when McCarthy comes out of the teacher's cafeteria I lock eyes with him immediately.

"Layla?" he says.

I look down at the floor. "Just put one foot in front of the other," Mom says. We walk past McCarthy, who calls out my name again. He sounds genuinely concerned, and I feel bad. But if I don't get to Belzer's office soon and get this off my chest, it will crush me.

I've just finished explaining to Belzer as best I can why I lit my assignments on fire when there's a knock on the door. Without waiting for an answer, McCarthy is standing in the principal's office.

"Mr. McCarthy," Belzer says, "we are in the middle of a meeting. Can you please come back later?"

"I'm sorry to interrupt. I just wanted to find out if everything was okay. Layla abruptly left class today saying it was an emergency." McCarthy nods to Mom and Nick.

"Do you mind if Mr. McCarthy joins us?" Belzer asks, motioning McCarthy to a chair. "Layla has just explained that she intentionally set the fire in her locker—that it was not an accident as her friend Liza indicated this morning. If I am understanding her, this was a misguided attempt to erase her first semester's performance before the parent-teacher conferences."

I can feel the tears in my eyes, and Mom gently takes my hand. I look over at McCarthy and he looks almost as sad as I feel, his head bowed and his hands folded together in his lap.

"Layla, I wish you'd felt comfortable coming to talk with me instead. We could have figured out a way to approach this," McCarthy says.

"I'm sorry, Mr. McCarthy," I say. I'm sorry to have disappointed him, and Mom, and Nick. And *myself*.

"I can see that this is more complicated than a simple destruction of property. But there is still the matter of the vandalism of the lockers, as well as the decision with her friend to take the blame in her place. Those are both extremely serious matters, which can't be entirely explained away by whatever academic frustration Layla has experienced." I get it. Belzer's not a bad guy, but he's got a job to do.

Still, I feel my heart sink.

Mom, who has not said a word since we arrived, speaks up.

"Mr. Belzer, certainly we will pay for the damage Layla caused. And if you feel that detention or some other punishment is also appropriate, I have no objection. As to what went on between Layla and Liza, I think we need to leave that to the girls to work out."

There is some more back and forth, but my mind is so full I can't focus anymore. I hear Belzer tell Mom that the cost of repairing the lockers and paying back the students for their destroyed belongings is $2000, and Mom agrees to pay even though there is no way we have that kind of money lying around. I also hear McCarthy propose that instead of detention, I spend my study hall period in the learning center with Mrs. Hirsch.

When it's all over, Nick reaches out his hand to me and practically lifts me out of the chair. He musses the top of my head, something I never let him do anymore.

"C'mon, 'munk. Time to go home," he says.

Chapter Thirteen

The drive home is silent except for the sound of some empty soda cans banging around in the trunk of Nick's car. Neither Mom nor Nick says anything. They don't seem mad. More as if they don't really know where to go from here. I don't either.

When we get back to the house, Mom is the first out of the car. She can barely keep her eyes open, and I remember that she hasn't slept at all after her shift last night.

I guess I must look pretty wiped out myself.

"'munk, let's nap for a couple of hours. We can talk about all of this later," Mom says. It isn't a conversation I'm looking forward to, and I'm happy to delay it.

Nick's still in the driver's seat, motor running. "You coming in?" Mom asks.

"Nah. Too wired. I'll be back in a little while," he says, putting the car into reverse and backing out of the driveway. I wonder where he's going, but I'm so tired that I follow Mom inside without asking.

We both sleep until 5 p.m. and then, half awake, I hear Mom puttering around the kitchen. A few minutes later she calls up to me from the bottom of the stairs.

"'munk, I made grilled cheese. Come down and eat." I'm amazed at her ability to act like everything is normal. I'm not hungry and I'm tempted to pull the covers over my head, but I go downstairs. Mom has set the table for the two of us. Nick's car is back and I can hear music coming from his room. My stomach clenches as I realize that he's been excluded on purpose; this is an ambush. But I deserve it.

We both focus on our sandwiches. Mom makes killer grilled cheese. She uses sharp cheddar, not American cheese, and thick pieces of bread she cuts from a whole unsliced loaf. She fries it in butter until the cheese oozes and the bread is crispy and hot. You have to eat it right out of the pan and Mom dives in. I normally wolf down grilled cheese in what Mom calls a "very unladylike manner." Now, I manage only a few bites, the conversation we're about to have, hanging over me. When Mom finishes, I clear the table and sit back down.

"I thought Mr. Belzer was very fair, didn't you?" Mom asks.

"Yes," I answer.

"He seemed to understand that you really didn't mean for any of this to happen." I can tell by the way Mom is kind of poking around the edges of the issue that she's trying to ask me, without actually asking me, why I did this crazy thing. If I could explain it better than I already have, I would. But I can't. I move my eyes to the cactus plant that sits on the counter just behind and slightly to the right of Mom so I don't have to look at her.

"You know, 'munk, that kind of acting out is no way to solve a problem—even one that had you feeling desperate."

Mom is doing her best, but I just can't see how this discussion is helping anything. Anyway, I have a much bigger problem than Mom. I have to face Liza.

"May I be excused?" I ask.

Mom inhales sharply, like I've sucker-punched her. "Do you really feel like we're finished here?" she says.

I'm saved from answering by Nick, who comes bounding into the kitchen, sniffing at the air like a puppy.

"You made grilled cheese for 'munk and not for me?"

"There's other leftovers in the fridge. I have to finish getting ready for work," Mom says. She pushes her chair back and stands up. She opens her mouth as though she is going to say something else, maybe something important that will fix everything and make it all make sense. But instead, she shakes her head a little and walks out of the kitchen toward her bedroom.

Nick pulls out a casserole dish and puts it in front of my face. "What is this?" he asks.

"I'm not sure. Enchiladas?"

He pops it in the microwave. As it turns slowly on the tray, he pulls a fork from the silverware drawer.

"You better go see Liza when Mom leaves," he says. He takes the casserole and puts it on the counter and stands there, eating directly from the dish.

"I'm going, although that's about as much of a plan as I have," I admit.

"You'll know what to say when you see her. She's your best friend."

Some friend I've been. But Nick's words give me courage.

When Mom leaves, I wait a couple of minutes just in case she comes back for something—I haven't been officially grounded, but I'm pretty sure I'm not supposed to be out. Then I get on my bike and ride slowly to Liza's. I let the five-minute trip take me ten, hoping that by the time I arrive I'll come up with a proper apology, if there is such a thing for this sort of treachery.

I arrive just as Liza's family is sitting down for dinner, forgetting that normal people don't eat as early as our family does so Mom can get to work. When Liza's mom answers the door, she looks at me a little funny before forcing a small smile and inviting me in.

"Layla, I'll set you a plate." Her mom is already at the cabinet pulling out another placemat when Liza interrupts.

Calm, although definitely not happy to see me, Liza doesn't say "hi." She glares at me while she talks to her mom.

"She didn't come here to eat. We'll be upstairs," Liza says. I follow her obediently to her room. I've spent so many hours hanging out here, but this time I'm scared. When we get inside, she closes the door behind me. I'm trying to think of what to say when Liza starts talking.

"So I lied to the principal and to my parents about accidentally setting the fire, and then you go and tell everyone that my lie was a lie? It was bad enough that I pretended to be so stupid that I would do a science experiment in my locker, but then you have to tell everyone that I wasn't telling the truth? Why couldn't you just leave it alone?" Liza's not yelling, but she's pink in the face and she's stomping back and forth between her bed and her desk, practically pinning me against the wall.

I don't say anything. I can't believe that what's ticking Liza off isn't that I was going to let her take the fall for me, but that I couldn't go through with it. It's all so turned upside down that I can't think straight. I take a deep breath and try to conjure what Nick would tell me if he were here.

Just tell her you're sorry for everything.

So I do.

"I came here to tell you how sorry I am. I never should've thought it was okay to let you try to save me.

And I'm sorry if I made it worse by coming clean with Belzer. Setting the fire was stupid, but what I did agreeing to let you take the blame was a million times worse. I really hope you'll forgive me."

Liza listens patiently without interrupting me until I stop talking. Mom was right. Facing Liza is much worse than any punishment Belzer could have handed me. I feel like my whole world is on the line as I wait for her reaction. And then she grants my wish.

"Okay, Layla. I forgive you. I'm going to eat dinner. I'll see you tomorrow." And just like that, Liza walks out of her room and down the stairs, into the dining room where her family is waiting for her.

I follow her down the stairs, walk out the door, and get on my bike. I make it about two blocks before I burst into tears.

Chapter Fourteen

"Thanks for stopping in, Layla," McCarthy says when I walk into his classroom. Like I had a choice. I have study hall in a couple of minutes, and I have to report to the Student Learning Center, but McCarthy emailed me to come here first. So here I am.

"Okay. I don't want to be late for Mrs. Hirsch," I say. The truth is, I don't want to go to Mrs. Hirsch at all. I don't know why I belong with the kids with issues. Everything has spiraled out of control since the stupid fire. At least things are almost normal with Liza now, and it's good to have Nick back on my team.

"Just sit for a moment," McCarthy says. He's the best teacher I've had in middle school, one of the few that doesn't think I'm hopeless. Probably the stunt I pulled has changed his mind, although he seems less disappointed in me now than he did when we were in Belzer's office yesterday. He smiles at me, and it isn't a sad smile, I don't think.

"So hear me out, okay? I'm not an expert in this, so I've arranged with Mrs. Hirsch to do some diagnostic testing with you," McCarthy says.

"An expert in what?" I ask. I don't like where this is going, but I trust McCarthy. I try to keep attitude out of my voice.

"An expert in learning differences. I'm pretty sure that you have a reading disorder that's been overlooked. If we can figure out the issue, and also let you complete your assignments with less time pressure, I think you'll do so much better. Really reach your potential. I think you'll be great."

McCarthy smiles again, confident that he's delivered good news. I'm less sure, even though I know he's the only teacher who has ever thought my bad grades didn't mean I was stupid or lazy.

"What does that mean, a reading disorder? I know how to read." I'm sure I sound defensive, but I feel like McCarthy is accusing me of something.

"Well, as I've said, I don't know for sure, but I would bet money you have some form of dyslexia. Obviously, you can read—so it isn't super serious. But the time it takes you to get through the text, and the way you struggle to get words down on paper in a way that matches what you are thinking in your head, suggests that something is different in the way your brain processes the written words. And Layla," he said, looking at me until I raised my eyes from the floor, "you've got it all in there. We just have to find the right key to unlock it."

I want to believe McCarthy, but at the same time I want him to be 100% wrong. It would be awesome to discover that there's actually a reason why letters sometimes refuse to stay put in words on the page, or why I can't keep straight the most basic spelling rules, or why it can take me half an hour to read through the same five pages that Liza is finished within ten minutes. But do I really want the explanation to be that there's some disconnect in my brain?

If I don't get up now and get moving, I will definitely be late for Mrs. Hirsch, but I feel glued to my seat. McCarthy, on the other hand, is pumped—like he's figured it all out, and he's here to save me.

"C'mon, Layla. I'll walk you down there," he says. He's halfway out the door by the time I get up, pick up my backpack, and follow him.

I've never been inside the Student Learning Center before. McCarthy strides in several steps ahead of me. He looks so confident and hopeful that it's almost contagious, but not quite. I cross the threshold slowly, as if I might be sucked into some kind of vortex, never to emerge into the world of normal students again.

From just inside the doorway I look around at the handful of kids sitting at desks in different parts of the room. There are a bunch of younger kids that I don't know. But then I see three eighth graders. Liam, who is so antsy that he spends half the period doing jumping jacks at the back of the classroom, completely unable to sit still for more than five minutes at a time. Melissa, who often stands too close when she talks to me and sometimes traps me in conversation when I'm trying to get to the bathroom or the water fountain. And Oliver, who's really smart but wears glasses about two inches thick and makes sure to tell everyone he's legally blind.

Oh my God. *What am I doing here?*

Then I see him, sitting in the corner, speaking in hushed tones with Mrs. Hirsch as she looks through his planner and pulls notebooks and texts out of his backpack, showing him each as she goes. Sammy.

"Oh, Layla, welcome," Mrs. Hirsch says, touching Sammy lightly on the shoulder before walking over to where I'm now standing in the entrance to the room with McCarthy. I haven't taken my eyes off Sammy. He smiles and waves at me, as if we've just run into each other in the hallway and not here, in this crazy place. I want to go over to him and find out why on earth he's here, but McCarthy is setting up a place for me to sit near the front, and Mrs. Hirsch has put some papers on the desk. There's no way for me to make a break for Sammy now.

"Please, come sit down, Layla," Mrs. Hirsch says. McCarthy takes that as his cue to leave. He gives me one more encouraging smile and a little salute, and walks out the door. If I didn't know Sammy was still there, I'd have followed McCarthy right out of the room, detention, or no detention. But somehow Sammy's presence, even if totally mysterious, calms me.

Mrs. Hirsch pulls out a sheet of paper with several paragraphs of different lengths on it and multiple-choice questions underneath each passage. At the top it says, "Progressive Reading Evaluation Tool," although it takes me several minutes to work that out with Mrs. Hirsch watching me. I slide the paper away from me and say, "What's this about? I can read, you know." I feel like a broken record, but does everyone really think I can't read? As much as I feel the temptation to believe that someone can help me, it's also insulting that they all think I belong back in first grade.

"I know you can, Layla," Mrs. Hirsch says. She sounds kind and not critical. "But I also know sometimes you struggle."

"So? Is there some magic wand you can wave over me and turn me into Liza?" I don't know why I just said that, and I immediately regret it. This doesn't have anything to do with Liza.

"I'm not interested in turning you into anyone else. I want to make reading and all your school work more rewarding for you," Mrs. Hirsch says.

I nod, afraid that if I try to speak my voice will get stuck in my throat.

"But first we have to know why you are having some difficulty. This test can give us a preliminary idea, and we can take it from there, if you're willing. Mr. McCarthy thinks it's a good idea," Mrs. Hirsch adds.

No teacher has ever taken an interest in me like McCarthy, and I have a flashback to Kyle claiming that he's some sort of pervert. But I know it isn't true. He really wants to help. I slide the paper in front of me and begin the evaluation.

When the bell rings, Mrs. Hirsch returns to where I am sitting still poring over the test. "There's no time limit to this, Layla. I'd like to see how you do when we remove the time pressure from you. When you come back tomorrow, you can continue."

"Okay," I say. Wow. That's a first. The idea that I can keep working until I actually finish is kind of shocking. I'm still thinking about it when Sammy comes up from behind me and puts his hands over my eyes.

"Guess who?" he says.

"Stop it, you moron!" I was so absorbed in the test that I had almost forgotten he was even in the room.

"What are you doing in here?" I ask.

"Executive functioning deficit," Sammy says.

"What's that?"

"It means I'm very disorganized and I can't keep stuff straight, to the point where it interferes with my learning. I forget to write down assignments, my locker is a disaster, I lose my textbooks. I'm sort of a mess," he says. shrugging. But he doesn't sound sad about it.

"How come I haven't noticed any of that? And why didn't I know you come here?" I ask.

"First of all, it's no big deal. Kids come here for all sorts of reasons. And Mrs. Hirsch helps me. I've been coming here since sixth grade. She teaches me ways to stay on top of stuff. And she goes through my planner, helps me organize my locker and my backpack, generally makes order out of chaos. She's the greatest," Sammy gushes.

At dinner, I tell Mom and Nick about what McCarthy said, and about my time in the Student Learning Center with Mrs. Hirsch. Instead of being happy, Mom seems kind of sad, which confuses me.

"Really? How could I have missed that? I feel guilty, 'munk. It makes me feel like a bad mother." I can see that she really means it, she's not just saying the words. I don't know how to respond. Should she have realized something was wrong? When I don't say anything to try to make her feel better, Nick does.

"It doesn't matter now, Mom. 'munk is going to get some help, and it's all going to be fine. There's no point in beating yourself up about something you didn't do on purpose. You have a lot of stuff you're dealing with. Now we move forward." Nick sounds just like the basketball coaches he admires—point out the positive, minimize the negative, forge ahead. I admire his attitude. I hope he's right.

After we finish eating I ask to be excused and I go over to Sammy's house. I ring the doorbell and Sammy answers, as if he were expecting me.

"Do you want to ride our bikes to the ice cream store?"

"I thought you'd never ask," he says. He grabs his helmet from the mud room and meets me outside with his bike. It's only a five-minute ride, but it's way too cold to be out, and definitely crazy to be having ice cream. Except it's never too cold for ice cream, really.

We leave our bikes lying on the grassy patch next to the sidewalk and we go into the store. Sammy orders an enormous waffle cone with three scoops of pistachio ice cream. I order a single scoop of vanilla chocolate chip in a cup. We sit down at one of the little tables. It feels like a date since it is just the two of us. I smile at Sammy and I can tell he's thinking the same thing.

"You know one of the things I like best about you?" I say to Sammy.

"Nope. Tell me."

"I like that you are always up for anything. Like, I could've knocked on your door and said let's go take the garbage to the dump, and you'd have that same smile on your face as you did when I asked you to get ice cream."

"I guess I just like being around you. I was happy to see you in the Student Learning Center today," Sammy says.

"I was happy to see you there too," I admit.

"You want to know something I really like about you?" Sammy asks.

"Yes." Because honestly, I sometimes wonder what he sees in me.

Sammy takes several licks of his ice cream cone before answering. When he speaks, he sounds serious.

"I like that you really think about stuff. You don't take things for granted—you try to be happy with what you have, but you also try to make things better. You try to make yourself better. You're inspiring." Sammy returns to attacking his ice cream.

I know I should stay quiet, but Sammy's good thoughts about me make me want to confess some bad thoughts I've had about him.

"Would it be wrong to tell you something about you that I don't like?"

"No—go ahead," Sammy says.

"I don't like how perfect your family is. You never seem to have any real problems. No relatives who are deadbeats, bills you can't pay, or loud arguments that I can hear from across the street." I feel mean-spirited, but I also feel relieved to have gotten it off my chest.

Sammy stops eating his ice cream and looks down at his sneakers for a second before fixing his eyes directly on mine.

"Every family has its problems. Maybe ours aren't that obvious to you, but they're there. You didn't know that I have things I need to work on until you saw me today in the Student Learning Center. Everyone has something to deal with, Layla."

Sammy is surprisingly wise for someone so goofy.

"Want to know something I don't like about you?"

I brace myself.

"I don't like how you keep all your opinions to yourself." Sammy makes a gesture like he's zipping his lips. I'm puzzled for a second, and then we both laugh.

Chapter Fifteen

McCarthy's in the front of the classroom doing that thing he does where he half sits on the edge of the desk and half stands. He's saying something, but I can't focus. Liza's in her regular seat next to me. She said "hi" when she came in, but there's no way to know if it was "hi, everything's cool, let's just go back to the way things were before," or "hi, you're that girl who used to be my best friend but now everything is different." My stomach hurts, and the pain is drowning out McCarthy. Then he starts talking about our new reading assignment, and some words filter through.

"We're reading 'Number The Stars' as part of the Holocaust unit at the same time your social studies class will be learning about World War Two," McCarthy says. "The novel is aimed at kids a little younger than you are, so the reading itself shouldn't be that challenging." I have a sudden thought that McCarthy's picked this book so I'll be able to handle it. I think everyone's looking at me, and

I feel a rush of anger and embarrassment. But then I remember that all the eighth grade English classes are following the same syllabus. Nick's always telling me I'm paranoid. Maybe he's right.

"The message is right on target for all of you. It's based on the true story of how the people of Denmark saved Copenhagen's Jewish population from Hitler. But it's also a universal story of a remarkable friendship between two young women and what they're willing to do for each other in unimaginable circumstances." McCarthy walks up and down the aisles, handing a book to each of us.

"I'd like you to pair up. You're going to discuss the book with your partner instead of me directing the discussion in class. I'm trusting you here. I'm not going to grade you or even be able to tell that you talked about the book instead of watching tv. But I think it's a valuable experience to see what it's like discussing a work of literature with a peer. You won't always be students. As adults you'll need to know how to talk about books with your friends."

On any other day, my hand would have shot up, making sure to claim Liza as my partner before anyone else had the nerve or the speed to choose her. And on any other day, Liza would have raised her hand at nearly the same instant—maybe not as urgently, but still—securing that we'd be together. Sometimes, McCarthy switches us up when we pick partners, but he seems to believe that if kids are happy working together, they will get more out of the assignment. He's cool that way.

But today, fear is tickling the back of my throat. What if I raise my hand and pick Liza, and she sits, with her hand planted firmly in her lap? What if I say, "I choose Liza," and McCarthy asks her if that's alright, and she says no? I glance at Liza out of the corner of my eye, and she's sitting still. Several pairs of students have formed, and McCarthy is writing them down on the smart board so he can keep track and make sure no one is left out. My arm is frozen at my side.

Then, in my peripheral vision, I see Liza raise her hand. I feel my face flush. Only when I hear her say, "I'd like to work with Layla," do I let myself turn and look at her. I'm smiling from ear to ear and I'm sure everyone thinks I'm deranged, but I'm so happy. Sammy taps the back of my chair with his foot in secret applause. In the back of the room Kyle says to no one in particular, "Looks like someone has a girl crush." Callie laughs, but no one else does. Maybe the other kids understand what a great moment this is. McCarthy does, for sure, but he doesn't let on—he just writes our names down, Liza and Layla, just like everyone else's.

Liza takes the bus home with Sammy and me, and the three of us sit on my front porch for a while. "What should we do on Monday?" Sammy asks.

"What's Monday?" I say.

"Martin Luther King Day—no school," Liza says. She tips her head back and takes in the weak rays of sun on this unusually warm January day.

We all know we'll end up staying home and watching TV—there's nothing much to do around here. Still, it's fun to talk about a day of freedom and pretend to make plans. And it feels great just to be sitting outside. After a few more minutes of fake sunbathing, Liza keeps us in line, as usual.

"Let's go inside, Layla; I think we should start reading the book for McCarthy's class."

"Yes, ma'am," I say, saluting, but I'm only kidding. Right now, I want nothing more in the world than to do homework with Liza. "Go on up to my room—just try to be quiet. My mom's still sleeping."

Sammy reluctantly stands up, making a show of lazily stretching his arms way over his head and yawning while he waits for Liza to go into my house. When she does, he comes closer to me and pokes me playfully in the ribs.

"See you later?" he asks.

"Maybe," I say. Not because I don't want to—I do. What's still so surprising is that *he* wants to. I'm not too good at playing hard to get, and I smile. Sammy looks as happy as if I'd just handed him a driver's license and the keys to a new car. He practically skips down the steps, and then he's gone.

I head into the house, stopping in the kitchen to pick up a big bag of potato chips, a couple of snack-size packets of M&Ms, and two cans of coke.

"I can't believe you're allowed to eat this stuff up in your bedroom. My mom doesn't let us take any food out of the kitchen," Liza says.

"With what goes on in Nick's bedroom, I think this is the least of her worries," I say. "Besides, M&Ms melt in your mouth, right?" I scarf a handful, and wash it down noisily with my Coke.

Liza looks at me as she carefully eats the chips, making sure not to scatter bits of crunchy goodness on my comforter.

"So you really like Sammy, hey?" she tosses out, real casual.

"Of course. Everyone likes Sammy," I say. I try to take the bag of chips from her, but she moves it out of my reach and hugs it to her chest.

"I don't mean you're going to get married, but you *like* like him," she teases.

I think about protesting, and then realize there's no point. "Yeah, I do."

"And he *like* likes you. That's so sweet," Liza says. Coming from anyone else, I would think she was making fun of me. But I know Liza means it—she thinks it's nice that I like Sammy and Sammy likes me.

"I guess," I say.

"You can hang out together in the Student Learning Center," Liza says, as if that's a cool destination where people who *like* like each other go to spend time.

"How'd you know Sammy goes there? I only found out when I saw him."

"I don't think he keeps it a secret, but I've known for a long time. Before he got linked up with Mrs. Hirsch, he used to ask me all the time for our homework assignments, or what books he should take home, or to help him find stuff in his locker. Do you remember what his locker looked like in sixth grade?"

Liza rolls her eyes but also smiles at the memory. In sixth grade, to me, Sammy was just the boy who lived across the street with the perfect family. I never saw the inside of his locker, and I don't think we ever had a conversation. I have a pang of jealousy that Liza was friends with Sammy first and that he used to ask her for help. Then I think, if I needed help, I'd ask Liza too. Always have.

"Come on, let's start," Liza says. We each take our "Number the Stars" and lie on my bed, stretched out head to toe, me on my stomach, Liza on her back with her head on my pillows. I'm so happy like this I feel it pulsing through me.

I'm reading at a snail's pace, as usual, but now making sure to take as much time as I need to puzzle stuff out as the words continue to play musical chairs on the page. I feel calmer, knowing that it's totally fine for me to read as slowly as I need to, that no buzzer is going to ring and no one is going to rip the book out of my hands with a loud "time's up!" Still, I've only read a couple of pages and I can hear Liza turning hers at a steady clip. I pull off her sock to get her attention.

"Hey, what're you doing?" she squeals.

"You know Mrs. Hirsch says that it's possible that once they figure out exactly what my language processing issues are, I might learn to read faster. Maybe I'll read faster than you."

"That would be great," Liza says.

"Nah, I'm sure that won't happen. But I do hope things get better. I feel like they will." I carefully put Liza's sock back on her foot. "Your feet stink!" I say, holding my nose.

"They do not!" She draws her knees in and tucks her feet protectively under her.

"No, of course they don't."

Liza's not perfect, I remind myself, but she would never walk around with smelly feet. We read in silence for a while, the horror and the hope of the friendship between Annemarie and Ellen filling our heads.

I hear Mom come out of her bedroom, and she knocks on my door.

"Come in," I say, although I'm finally in the groove with the book and I'm a little afraid to stop.

"Hi, girls," Mom says. "Can I get you a snack?" Then she notices the chips and empty M&Ms packs on my bed and she shakes her head a little. "I guess you already helped yourself," she says. But she's not mad. "It's kind of close to dinner, anyway."

"Is it? I better go," Liza says. Mom leaves my room and heads downstairs as Liza gets up and slips her book into her backpack.

"Hey, Liza? Can I ask you something?" I sit up on my bed, smoothing out the comforter in the space Liza has vacated.

"Sure," she says.

I try to talk but my voice feels strangled inside me. I take a deep breath, and exhale my question in a rush of words. I realize at that moment that the thought has been churning inside me since I spoke with McCarthy about Mrs. Hirsch and the Learning Center.

"Do you think if they fix my learning differences, I'll be someone else? Like I won't be me anymore?"

Liza sits back down on my bed. "Of course you'll be you, silly. You'll be you, but even better."

Something about Liza's confidence is contagious, and I feel the weight I've been carrying lift a little. "Okay, if you say so," I manage. I want to hug her, but I'm afraid that too big a show of emotion will overwhelm her. We're still in a delicate place.

"Well I do say so," Liza says. "Listen, I have to go or my mom will send out a search party." I hear her say "hi" to Nick as they pass on the stairs. Then he's in my doorway.

"Hey, 'munk. You okay? You look a little dazed and confused," Nick says.

I smile. "No, I'm good. I'm just reading this book. It's kind of intense." I open to the page where I left off, and I burrow under my comforter. Nick's halfway out my door when I call to him.

"Hey, bro, thanks for helping me with Belzer and Mom and Liza and everything."

"Don't sweat it, 'munk. Just take it slow." Nick walks out of my room, and I hear him gently close the door to his.

I open the book and start to read again.

Chapter Sixteen

When I come down for dinner, I can tell right away something's up. Mom's made fried chicken cutlets and rice pilaf and set the table, but instead of looking relaxed like she usually does on days when she has the time to cook and eat with us, she's standing with her back against the fridge, arms crossed over her chest. She has something in her hand, and when I sit down she says, "This came for you," and pushes an envelope at me.

"Wow," I say. I don't get mail. Who writes letters? Then I see "Jeff" printed neatly on the upper left-hand corner, and I understand why Mom looks tense.

"It came today. Any idea what he wants?" she says.

"No," I say. "I haven't seen him or talked to him since Thanksgiving when you told me I wasn't allowed to have anything to do with him."

"Well, you've been known to break the rules, young lady."

She doesn't need to remind me. I've apologized a million times for the locker thing. She knows how bad I feel about it. I thought we were beginning to move on, but maybe this letter from my dad has set us back.

I'm about to ask if I can be excused so I can go up to my room and read my letter in private, even though we haven't eaten yet, when Nick comes lumbering into the kitchen. His knee isn't 100% yet, but it's good to see him moving around more easily. He also has more purpose these days, like he's re-entered his own life, and mine too.

"What you got there, 'munk?" he says, sitting down and starting to pile his plate with food. His appetite has never suffered.

"What she has is a letter from Jeff," Mom answers for me. She pulls out a chair and sits down, and it's clear I'm going nowhere. "Please open it," she says.

I look at the envelope and notice that there's no return address, just his name. I wonder if he's hiding from me, or from Mom, or whether he has nowhere he calls home. I pull a single piece of paper out of the envelope, and before I start reading I'm already sad that the letter is so short. Jeff's handwriting and spelling are even worse than mine, and combined with my improving, but still lousy reading skills, it's pretty slow-going. But I'm determined to get through it myself before sharing with Mom and Nick, so I let them sit while I take my time.

Dear Layla,

If you're reading this, I guess your Mom said it's okay, and I'm glad. Hope you can make out my handwriting.

I heard about your troubles in school, and about what happened with the lockers. For what it's worth, I understand how things are for you, although I'm not excusing your behavior. I also had—hell, still have—a learning issue that has made it hard for me my whole life. I know how it probably makes you feel different and lonely sometimes, like you just don't fit in with the other kids. Anyway, that's how it makes me feel, and those feelings were even stronger when I was your age. I can definitely understand the frustration that would lead you to do something crazy, like set those papers on fire.

Maybe you already know that these kinds of learning issues can be inherited—I'm afraid that might be the biggest thing I've given you (besides your beautiful name). The difference between you and me is that you have the chance to work hard and change how this affects you, so it doesn't hold you back. I want you to grab that chance.

Believe in yourself and be proud of who you are, because your mom and I believe in you and are proud of you. We might not agree on much, but we agree on that.

I quit my job at McSweeney's. I think it's probably best for everyone if I leave town. I will let your mom know where I land, so if you want to be in touch and she says it's okay, you'll know how to find me.

Please find in this envelope a check made out to your school for $1000. I wish I could pay off the whole debt, but this is the best I can do. I hope it helps.

Chin up, young lady. You have a bright future ahead of you.

Love,

Jeff (Dad)

When I finish reading, I put the letter down on the table and reach over to grab a tissue from the countertop. I'm not crying, but I feel like I should be prepared in case I start. It's weird that my dad can understand this huge thing about me when he hasn't ever been a part of my life. It makes me feel close to him and distant all at the same time.

"Are you going to let me read that?" Mom asks. She has her hand out for the letter—not prying, exactly, but definitely concerned. I hand it to her while I pull out the check from the envelope. Mom takes it out of my hand so fast it almost gets torn in half.

"He can't buy his way into your life, 'munk," Mom says quietly. She's looking at the check though, and I can tell she's relieved.

"I don't think that's what he's trying to do," I say.

"How did he even know what happened at school, or how much money we owe? Did you speak to him? Sneak out of here to meet him?" Mom seems like she's trying to sound angrier than she is—like when Nick or I leave the milk out all night after a midnight cereal run and she has to throw away practically a whole gallon in the morning.

Angry, but not deep-down angry.

"I didn't, I swear—"

"'munk didn't talk to him," Nick says between mouthfuls. "I did. I thought he should know what's going on. I told him to man up and take some responsibility for his family," he says.

"You did that?" I ask. "Like mano a mano?" I think this isn't exactly the right context, but I've always wanted to say it. Nick smiles, and even Mom purses her lips, like she's holding back.

And then we are all smiling, and I start to giggle. What starts out kind of nervous gets louder and stronger, until we are all laughing hard and I never want it to stop.

When it finally dies down, Mom takes my hand across the table. "'munk," she says, "I just want to say that—"

"Mom," I say, gently but firmly, "I don't want to be called 'munk, anymore. My name is Layla."

She smiles.

Epilogue

"I can't do this," I say.

Nick pulls his car up in front of the high school and kills the engine. It's a warm June day, and his AC doesn't work so the windows are all cranked open. But there's hardly anyone around. Who comes to school voluntarily on a Saturday morning?

"Of course you can do this, Layla," Nick says. "You're so ready. You know this stuff cold." Nick punches me on my upper arm, but gently so he won't hurt me. "Go get 'em!"

I smile weakly at him and reach for the door handle. McCarthy has convinced me to take the entrance exam for ninth grade Honors English for the coming school year. I get extra time now under state law because of the dyslexia, and I've been working really hard on the material and my skills with Mrs. Hirsch. Still, I'm crazy nervous that I will bomb the test and have to admit to everyone that I'm not any better than I was before.

"I'm scared."

"Everyone's scared sometimes. You know how scared I was to get out there on the basketball court again, even after the docs told me my knee was good to go? I was terrified. But I knew you and mom were there for me, no matter what. Hell, even Jeff showed up. You're going to be great, Layla."

I feel calmer and I give his repaired knee a little squeeze.

"Hey, Nick? Sometimes, could you still call me 'munk? I kind of miss it."

"You got it," he says. "Now get out of here or you'll miss your test."

I close the door, pump my fist in the air, and run up the stairs.

Acknowledgments

I began working on *My Name Is Layla* in 2017 as part of a workshop entitled "Writing for Youth" at The Writing Institute at Sarah Lawrence College. At the time, I was excitedly awaiting the publication of my debut women's fiction novel, *Unreasonable Doubts*, a legal thriller and love story inspired by my career as a public defender. I'd never considered writing for children and I had no idea what I would write. Two semesters later, I had a draft of *Layla*, a new chapter written each week and critiqued by an insightful teacher and a wonderful and supportive group of writing colleagues. A huge thank you to my teacher, Wendy Townsend, and to my classmates, Carolyn Lyall, Jean Huff, Michelle Gewanter, Alison Cooper-Mullen, Laura Sinko, Elyse Pollack, Rebecca Adams, and Suzanne Ste. Therese. This book would not exist without your enthusiasm and guidance.

Several other friends were early readers who helped *Layla* develop. Thank you to Rosalind Citron, Jill Katz, Nate Katz, Emily Segal, and especially Dvora Rabino.

I am thrilled to be published by TouchPoint Press. Thank you to Sheri Williams and Ashley Carlson for giving me this opportunity, and a special shout out to Jennifer Haskin for her thoughtful and kind editing—you brought out the best in *Layla*.

Thank you to all my family and friends who continue to encourage me to write and to try new avenues. Your positivity is very much appreciated.

Finally, I want to thank Pierre, Ariella, and Micah. There's no better squad in the world.

About the Author

Author photo by Ayelet Feinberg

REYNA MARDER GENTIN lives with her husband and children in Westchester County, New York. Reyna's first novel, *Unreasonable Doubts*, a romantic legal thriller inspired by her work as a public defender, was a finalist in the Women's Fiction Writers Association Star Award for debut fiction and you can find it at bit.ly/UnreasonableDoubts. Reyna studies at The

Writing Institute at Sarah Lawrence College and her short stories and personal essays have been published widely online and in print. You can find out more by visiting reynamardergentin.com. If you'd like to arrange a visit to your school, please contact me at reyna@reynamardergentin.com.

If you enjoyed this book, I would be honored to read your review on Goodreads, Amazon, Barnes and Noble, and/or one of the major online retail platforms.